Jonathan Sturak

From Vegas

With Blood

Tales of love, mystery, and suspense

Also by Jonathan Sturak

NOVELS

A Smudge of Gray

Clouded Rainbow

To RV

About the author:

Jonathan Sturak grew up in the Pocono Mountains of Pennsylvania. He is a Penn State University graduate and holds degrees in Computer Science and Film. He currently lives in Las Vegas where he uses the energy of the city to craft stories about life and the human condition. *The Place Called Home*, Sturak's essay about Eastern European heritage in Northeast PA, was featured on *Glass Cases*, associate literary agent Sarah LaPolla's pop culture blog at bigglasscases.blogspot.com. His debut thriller novel *Clouded Rainbow* was published in December 2009 and has over 100,000 downloads on the Amazon Kindle. New for 2012 is his psychological thriller novel, *A Smudge of Gray*. Sturak keeps updated information on his website at sturak.com

From Vegas

With Blood

Kiosk on the Strip
7:02 p.m.

So, you're new here, huh? I'm Daniela. Welcome to the worst job in the world. You do know that you're selling T-shirts to tourists, right? Well come on. Don't just stand there. Come here. I'll show you the cart. Since it's your first day, you get no commission. I know it sucks, but that's the company's policy. These Israeli businessmen are tough bosses.

You see these T-shirts—these one hundred flavors of "I Love Las Vegas" and "Hoover Dam"? Well, you need to get those people to reach into their pockets to pull out five dollars. But that's not it; we must up-sell! That's what Amit says. He hired you, right?

Twenty thousand people walk by here every day—twenty thousand suckers. You're new to Las Vegas too, huh? Well, welcome to Sin City. Did I mention that this is the worst job in the world?

I can only work at night, and I've tried everything. I was a cocktail waitress for a while, but I was fired for throwing a gin and tonic in a sleazeball's face. After that, I was a go-go dancer. That was fun, but I got tired of the cheap pick-up lines. I still like to dance when I'm bored, which is pretty often. Kiosks are my thing now. I've sold everything from knock-off designer purses, to fake jewelry, to bogus hair removal kits. The rule with these jobs is the same—push, push, push.

Some suckers stop to buy T-shirts, while some stop to try to buy me. Mostly the drunk yuppies. Ha! I remember one guy showed me one of these porno cards littering the Strip and swore that I was the girl. She did look like me, but I don't have stars for nipples.

Four more hours of this, and then the night is ours. You want to know when you get paid? They hold the first check. You have to wait for four weeks. Why is it you want to work here again? You should run away now. This job's not much, I know, but we all have a little side business in Vegas. Nothing is as it seems. In fact, tonight I have a gig after work. Why don't you tag along? I'll introduce you to my friends. I like you. You're quiet.

I'm bored. I already sold my quota for today. Let's take a break. What do you want to do? What's that in my bag, you ask? Ah... That is a very special book. That's what I read when I'm bored. Check out the first story. Go on. The first one always rolls over me.

A Brush of Love

My name is Anne Daniels. I'd like to tell you a story—a story about life, about love, and about...well...I don't want to get ahead of myself. Three summers ago, I started a job in Indianapolis as a secretary for a small law firm that handled insurance cases. Indiana was home for me. While I was born in southern Nevada, I was raised in the Hoosier State. The Midwest was my life, and my new job was something I could handle, something safe. I did the usual mundane office duties—answering the phone, signing for packages, and taking notes. It wasn't a bad job. In fact, I rather enjoyed it. Two partners ran the firm. My boss was Albert Bernstein, the old Jewish boy. You know, one who smoked those big stogies, talked through his nose, and always called others "kiddo" or "babe," even if they were only ten years younger. Mr. Bernstein was in his sixties and had the most obnoxious wife who would never even acknowledge my name when she called.

"My husband, please," she would say whenever I answered the phone.

My life at that time was starting to pick up. While my parents kept pushing me to go to college, I didn't want to go to school; I wanted to meet a man. You know, one of those new law boys fresh out of an Ivy League school. I was twenty-five and my new job seemed to be the right thing. While it was just a glorified secretary position, perhaps Mr. Bernstein would hire my future husband. But above all, I was a working woman now—a hopelessly available working woman, I might add.

Men and I were like water and oil. I was the water and they were the oil, and I always seemed to find the ones who were extra thick and highly flammable. I did have a boyfriend, one of those chatty computer nerds who always talked about his computer games and Star Wars collectibles. His name was Jeff and he was thick like motor oil.

A month into my job, Mr. Bernstein decided to take a trip to an insurance conference in Tampa, Florida. It wasn't the first time I saw him go away on business, but it was the first time he asked me to accompany him. Initially, I thought about making up some excuse not to go, but then I realized that I would only be fooling myself. Jeff and I needed some space and I only had my cat, Lucy, to worry about. So, I thought, *Sure, what the heck*, and gave my mom the kitty litter scooper. I was never in the Sunshine State and what better way to go than on a company paid trip.

We left on a Monday morning at six a.m. from Indianapolis. I overpacked, as if I were staying a week, but I had no idea what to expect. I packed everything from a sundress to a business suit—actually, three of each. Mr. Bernstein's plan was to stay at the same hotel as the conference. That way we could check-in, make the Monday afternoon sessions, and then prepare for the full day on Tuesday. Then we would catch the Tuesday evening flight back north. He said he'd traveled a million times, and for all I knew, he actually did.

This was the second flight in my life, the first being to Philadelphia when I was seven. While every jostle of the plane made my stomach sink, the tropical paradise underneath us brought it back up. As soon as we landed at the airport, Mr. Bernstein and I shared a cab to the hotel—the Doubletree on Cypress Street. As we made the five minute drive, a new world painted itself outside my cab window. Palm trees swayed; seagulls soared; and tourists marched. Florida was a beautiful state, a state which I had wished one day to visit. Now I was here, breathing the warm and humid July air, but all we were planning to do was stay hidden inside our hotel.

The first day at the conference was filled with mind-numbing seminars on proposed tort reform, new forms of insurance, and embracing technology to better a law practice. Mr. Bernstein had me take notes on everything while he drank coffee and smoked cigars with his old buddies. But I couldn't complain, this beat sitting in our office in Indianapolis doing the same thing. At least I had a room full of new faces to keep my heavy eyes moving.

At five o'clock, the conference was over. Mr. Bernstein asked me how my note taking went, and then informed me that we were having dinner in the hotel restaurant at six with a couple of attorneys from New York. When I glanced over his shoulder to see the two men, I hoped Pierce Brosnan's and Clive Owen's twin would massage my eyes, but all I witnessed was Ben Stein and Woody Allen gumming a stogie. The old men were one thing, but I was not in the mood to have dinner with choking smoke clouding the view of my plate. What could I say to Mr. Bernstein? All I could reply to his proposal was, "See you in the lobby at six."

I went up to my room, the only place of safety, and looked out the window at paradise. The afternoon sun lowered over the city as water vapor from a recent shower swirled over the macadam like mist over a placid lake. I craved to explore this land of lushness even if my only mode of transportation was my two feet. I needed to come up with an excuse, something to say to Mr. Bernstein to get out of our dull dinner. I looked around my room for an answer. I needed a pair of pliers large enough to remove this thorn in my side. As my eyes searched, I suddenly saw a way out—a bottle of Midol.

I called Mr. Bernstein's room and told him that I wasn't feeling well and that I wanted simply to stay in the room for the evening. He still tried to convince me to join him with his nasally rasp, but as soon as I mentioned the word "cramps," he told me to take care and that he would see me in the morning. With the cigar smoke extinguished for the evening, I finally had time to myself.

I showered and as I stepped from the bathroom with a towel wrapped around myself, I pondered how I should dress—something casual yet sexy, classy yet opportunistic, and local yet out-of-town. I perused my clothes, tossed aside my business suits, and beheld my sundresses—pink, blue, and light green. After contemplating the unknown night, the sun kissed flowers on the pink dress won me over. Shoes were my next issue, but I decided to wear a pair of red flats, stylish yet easy on the feet.

It was just after six o'clock as I left my room and wandered toward the front of the hotel, bypassing the restaurant. For some reason, I felt like I was committing a crime, sneaking out of prison on the lookout for cigar smoke. Finally, I broke free as the warm evening sun bathed me in light. I took a breath of fresh air, air that I craved to breathe since touching down earlier in the day. I could sense a dampness reach my lungs, a scent much different from the deciduous Indiana. I walked to the street and saw hotel after hotel lined on each side of the road. This was the business and tourist district, a district filled with travelers like myself—a district I wanted to break free from. I had two paths to continue my journey. I looked behind me, and then in front. Both distant cross streets looked the same, but I was sure both would lead toward very different locations. After seeing a group of suits crossing the street toward me, I made the decision to drift toward the only signal I had—the setting sun.

I reached the distant block as a whirlwind of activity greeted me. Cars raced on the road in front of a massive mall with shops and restaurants surrounding it. It appeared I had rolled the dice in my favor. Floridians flourished around me. I crossed the street and rested my eyes on a bakery café, JavaHut. It was a small, unimpressive establishment nestled between a tanning parlor and a pet groomer. The place had a local feeling, and at that point, I wanted nothing more than a taste of the local life.

I entered as the smell of fresh bread invigorated my senses. Families out for dinner and individuals savoring a book or newspaper filled the restaurant. This was the perfect place for me to unwind, to sit and listen, and nothing else. I ordered the turkey avocado on three-cheese bread with a baguette for the side.

After I poured some iced tea next to the fountain drinks, I looked for a place to sit. The café was bursting at the seams, but surely, I could find some place to rest my aching bones. Near the window, I saw three occupied tables next to each other, but as I took the first sip of iced tea, the middle couple took their last, leaving me with an empty spot.

I snagged the table and basked in the new world around me as I savored my turkey sandwich. A thirty-something woman bronzed by the sun entered pushing a baby carriage. Then, a few college-aged beach bums sporting board shorts flip-flopped in. I love people watching, studying the seemingly random strangers sharing the same random path as me.

A middle-aged married couple and what appeared to be their adolescent daughter sat to my right. The family was probably out for a night at the mall, but I didn't know; the only thing I did know was they appeared happy, content. As I indulged in my sandwich, the sound of legal jargon hit my ear. I glanced to my left and saw two men sipping coffee, trading words as if they were worth something. One man wore a loose black dress shirt, opened one too many buttons, and his partner wore a T-shirt plastered with USF on the front. Even though a crowd surrounded me, it seemed I could only focus on the two men's voices spouting insurance deductibles and proposed court dates. The man in the college shirt explained how he was at a traffic light and the guy in front of him stopped short. It was as if I were back with Mr. Bernstein, taking notes at one of his client's meetings. The only difference was my pen and steno pad had become a turkey on cheese bread.

I wondered what kind of attorney this was, meeting his client in a coffee shop. Was this to protect the client or the attorney? As their voices overwhelmed me, I knew I had to focus on something else, something around me. I glanced to my right to peek again at the daughter's cute smile, but she was gone. A void was present where she once was. Then, something hit me. My nose received a blast of something intoxicating. It was a masculine cologne, an aroma that took my breath away. I studied my peripheral vision and saw the silhouette of a man sitting next to me in the same spot as the girl's parents. They must have snuck away, replaced by this succulently scented man, as the attorney and his client had engulfed me.

I felt something come over me, something that drew me to this man. I wanted to turn and study him like an art historian studies the Mona Lisa, but I couldn't. I had to do it subtly, tactfully. As I started on the second half of my sandwich, I stole a peek. He wore a nonchalant pink Lacoste shirt and plaid shorts with sandals on his feet. The man seemed as cool as a cool breeze cutting through the moist Florida air.

While my glance lasted less than a second, I painted him in my mind as I turned back to my iced tea. I saw that his focus was on something in his hands, something that my glimpse failed to realize. I wanted to, in fact I needed to, glance again. As I turned slightly, I noticed a cup of coffee sitting in front of him, but the object consuming his attention drew me closer. He was drawing something with colored pencils in a sketchpad. It looked like his hand was creating a bird of some sort standing on a beach. I immediately stopped and focused on nothing other than the sketch his mind and his hands were creating.

Something about an artistic guy intrigued me, his gentle passion for his art in an ungentle world. I immediately wanted to know more about this guy. Who he was, where he lived, and where he came from. But as his hands drew the legs of the bird, I realized my glance had turned into a stare. I lifted my gaze toward his face, and as I did, his green eyes saw through me. I felt a bit embarrassed, but it was worth it. He had a look about him, the kind of look that flowed over you like a hand massaging your sore muscles. The Florida sun had tanned his warm face as just enough stubble coated it to tease me. I smiled as he returned the gesture with his own. I was bizarrely nervous as if I were back in high school in the presence of my crush. As my senses screamed not knowing what to do, what to say, he cut the tension by softly saying, "Hi there."

I asked him about his drawing as he proudly turned it to me. The sandy beach, the glowing sun, and the basking bird looked so simple yet complex sketched in colored pigment. I wondered whether this sight actually existed beyond his mind, somewhere hidden in the land around us.

He asked my name with his brawny voice and just as he devoted all of his attention to the drawing, he was now devoting all of his attention to me. I felt as if I were a drawing, crafted by the hands of this mysterious man. His name was Alex, and he moved to Clearwater Beach ten years ago on a full scholarship to the University of South Florida for a fine arts degree. He stayed, since the city of Clearwater and its wealthy residents loved his artwork depicting some of Florida's most beautiful treasures. As he explained his passion, he pointed to a nearby wall where there was a painting of a beautiful palm tree overlooking the beach. Without him even saying a word, I knew it was his.

"So what brings you here?" he asked as I slid a little closer to him.

I explained my situation—attending the conference with my boss, needing some time to get away, and my plan to leave tomorrow evening. Alex had a quality that was absorbing. He looked at me with his green eyes as if I were the only person in that overcrowded room.

"So does that location that you're drawing actually exist?" I asked as I finished my meal.

He didn't respond verbally, but he smirked in such a way that I knew, in fact, it did. It was a memory in his mind, a scene of tropical bliss that filled his senses. Suddenly, I too wanted to experience this location, this vivid place that I could escape to whenever I closed my eyes.

"I can take you there," he offered.

I stopped for a moment, thinking about the simple five words that his vocal cords vibrated. My brain said to keep my guard up, to be cautious of anyone known for less than ten minutes, but there was something telling me to go for it, to take the ticket to see the world that I craved. The things we don't do today we often regret tomorrow or even for the rest of our lives. Before my brain could fully weigh the pros and cons, my mouth released four simple letters forming a word, a word that would shape my night and my life forever.

"Sure."

"I have my moped. I'll show you Florida, and I'll have you back before your bedtime," he joked.

We stood up as he collected his drawing kit. Alex had to be at least six feet tall, tall enough to be noticed, but not enough to be mocked. I followed him out of the bustling establishment. He held the door for me as the balmy air surrounded us. I walked out of that café very differently than when I had entered. Alex led me across the parking lot, gripping my hand to scurry as one between the passing cars. His grasp felt warm, felt strong like a man in charge. I wondered how many other women felt the same power as I did. I remember just staring at him as he led me through the parking lot. He was so tall and his hair flowed in the wind. Then we arrived at his ride. It was a small red moped barely big enough for a kid, let alone a fisherman and his catch. But he assured me that this was the only way to travel through the Florida streets. Alex offered me his only helmet so I strapped it on. I was now concealed from being a secretary, replaced by a Florida girl on a bike.

Alex put his supplies in an attached pack, and then fired up the puny engine. The bike was corny, but corny in a good way. He commanded the miniature moped as I sat behind him and held his waist. Then, like a cowboy escorting the sheriff's daughter on an injured horse, we were off. The bike puttered through the lot as Alex dodged cars left and right. Even though we traversed the traffic with barely any defense, I took a whiff of his masculine scent and knew that I was protected.

We cut through the humid air as my senses overflowed with the life of Florida. Palm trees swayed in the breeze as traffic surged. The homes looked nothing like those in Indiana. Barrel roofs and colored stucco replaced the flat shingles and vinyl siding from the north.

We stopped at a traffic light as three business professionals crossed the street in front of us, a law office behind them at the street corner. The woman in the group wore a suit that was cool and classy. I studied her saunter, and then her face that brightened as she chuckled with the handsome middle-aged men accompanying her. I wondered how it would be working and living in a tropical land hidden away from Old Man Winter. The light turned green as we continued on our adventure. I didn't exactly know where we were going, but I knew that following the setting sun would eventually lead us somewhere.

After about twenty minutes of riding, signs for Clearwater Beach pointed us onward. Bikini clad women and shirtless men replaced the business professionals and locals navigating the streets. We were in the tourists' playground, far, far away from my hotel district. For a moment, I wondered what my cigar-puffing boss was doing, but the sight of the beach in front of me quickly removed him from my mind.

"Is that where we're going?" I shouted through the wind.

"No. That's where all the tourists go. We're going to a very special place," he replied.

He turned the bike northward as we drove away from the crab shacks and vacation motels. Exquisite beachfront homes filled our view as we drove further away from the mainstream. I was getting a tour of the Florida Gulf Coast that not even the tourists received. As the engine droned, Alex turned off the roadway and into a sandy path.

"We're almost there," he said, as I instinctively yelped from the abrupt change.

We jostled on the packed sand as more and more space separated the large homes. It was just the seagulls and us as we rode with the rolling ocean to our left. A small sand dune came into our view, and our path. My pupils dilated. There was no way we were going to make it.

"Hold on," Alex hollered as I gripped his waist even tighter.

He pegged the throttle; we popped over the hill through my girlish laughter. Then we slowed to a stop. I wondered whether something had happened to the moped. I looked around trying to assess the situation, but as I turned to the ocean, I knew exactly why we had stopped. Alex shut off the puny engine as the sound of paradise filled my ears. The picture he drew back at the café was now in front of me, its pencil strokes now full of life. The setting sun, rolling waves, and white sand soothed my sore senses. Seagulls squawked in the distance and landed around us to inspect the new life.

"What do you think?" Alex asked as he stepped off and helped me with my helmet.

"Breathtaking," I replied.

Alex removed his sandals and tucked them on the bike as I did the same. The white sand tickled my feet. Alex took my hand and led me slowly, softly toward the water in front of us. The image was awesome, one of the most awe-inspiring ever to enter my eyes.

"How did you find this place?" I asked.

His response still rings in my mind. "I love finding beautiful things in this world, including you."

He grasped both of my hands and looked at me with those eyes. And then, he leaned in and kissed me tenderly. I let go and gave myself to him. The waves pulsed; the seagulls fluttered; the sun burned. And there we were making love surrounded by it all. I felt like I was in a dream, whisked away by a prince sent to me by my subconscious. I couldn't think; I couldn't anticipate; I could only be. It felt like this was the real reason for my decision to go to Florida, a reason that would become a part of me so deeply, I couldn't think of my life without it.

Calmness consumed me, a deep contentment after our lovemaking. Alex grabbed his sketchbook and started to sketch, but all I wanted to do was to hold on to him and to bask in the remaining light. After the ocean finally stole the sun away, Alex offered me a ride back to my hotel, a ride back to reality. I wished I could stay and live a life with him, but I knew I could never do it. All I could do, however, was hold on to him as we rode through the night, hold on to him as tightly as I could.

We pulled into my hotel's parking lot, as the uneasy feeling returned. I wondered whether Mr. Bernstein was somewhere lurking in the shadows.

"Why don't you move to Florida?" Alex asked as he stopped near the hotel's entryway.

"I have a life back north."

"Life is about living, and I can see that you are alive here with me," he replied gently.

His words energized my soul. He was right. But could this work? Could I just pick up and move to a place that I had only dreamed of before?

"Will you take a chance with me?" he asked so softly I could barely hear his voice, yet I could hear it louder than anything.

I wanted to tell him that he had opened a side of me that I never knew existed, a side that wanted to move to Florida to become that businesswoman at the traffic light. But before I could reply, I saw thick black smoke spewing from an old car in the parking lot. The whirling pollution reminded me of cigar smoke—cigar smoke from my life in Indiana. I simply smiled at my prince as he took my hand and kissed it. Alex knew that what had happened was special, and just like a completed masterpiece, the artist must leave it untouched after the last brushstroke.

Alex reached into his moped's pack and handed me his sketch. I realized then what he had been doing as I relaxed on the sand back at the beach. He added me to the picture, lying in paradise. And then like that, he rode away toward the unknown as I simply watched darkness devour him.

I went to bed, and then began the second and last day of the conference bright and early. I saw Mr. Bernstein and he asked if I was feeling better. All I could respond was, "I'm fine." I continued my note taking over the humdrum insurance presenters. While my body was physically sitting next to my boss in the conference room, my mind was with Alex, back on that beach.

Later that evening we flew back north, and as the plane transcended paradise underneath us, I looked hard to find Alex and that beachfront, but I couldn't find it or him. The only place they existed now was in my mind.

We arrived back in Indianapolis, back to the status quo. Things were the same, my family, my job, my boyfriend, my monotonous life, but as the weeks went by, I craved more. I craved to return to Florida. As I stared at Alex's sketch day after day, I thought about his last words—his last question. I realized that I wanted to move to the Sunshine State and become my drawn counterpart. I wanted to live life.

Then, exactly one month after my trip, I decided to take action. I flew back to Tampa, back to the place that I couldn't get out of my mind. I wanted to search for Alex, to tell him of my aspirations, and to tell him that I wanted to be next to him. The only thing I had was his sketch that I kept close to my heart. I had no plan, no area of town to search, no idea of where to find him. All I could do was go back to the place of our meeting, go back to that café. Something told me that the answer I sought would be in there.

I walked in and looked around at those two tables where we had met, but all I saw was an elderly man and woman barely awake. My prince was nowhere to be found. I suddenly felt lost, defeated, but then I saw something that offered a glimmer of hope. It was Alex's painting hanging proudly on the wall—the painting of the palm tree. I saw a waitress cleaning a nearby table and I asked her, "Do you know this artist?"

"Alex?" she said.

"Yes, Alex. Do you know where I can find him?"

Her expression suddenly turned sour, as if I had delivered some terrible news. She paused for a moment, and then said something that would forever haunt me and forever change the way I think, the way I act—the way I live.

"He passed away three weeks ago. A truck hit his moped. It was all over the news in town."

My heart stopped as I filtered out of the store incapable of thinking. I went back to my hotel, packed my things, and then left Florida. As the Sunshine State disappeared from my plane's window, a part of my heart darkened, choked away from the light.

"How could he be gone? Why?" I asked myself repeatedly.

I felt terrible. If I had answered Alex's question in that parking lot, would the dice have rolled differently? I realized that I would forever regret that decision, regret not listening to my heart and not taking that chance.

It's been three years since this experience, and I still think about Alex and that evening on the beach. I still live in Indianapolis and work for Mr. Bernstein. Not much has changed, in fact. While I have accepted my life in Indiana, I often sit back and close my eyes where I can see Alex, see his tanned face, his cool hair, his green eyes, and his sparkling smile. While he is gone from this world, he lives on in my mind...and in my heart.

Aw... I love that story—so beautifully sad. I wish I could find a man. The guys I meet always leave a sour taste in my mouth. I would ask you about your relationships, but I don't want to dwell on the past. Las Vegas is a city that runs from its past. I remember a strip mall right here where we are standing. You know, it had a mom-and-pop convenient mart, a gift shop, and a place to buy discounted show tickets. I remember there was also a floral shop. They had some beautiful flowers, but then the city snuck up on the strip mall and bulldozed it to make way for this kiosk village. All these tourists are walking on the same spot that those beautiful flowers had once occupied, but these people have no idea; they are oblivious to what was once here. You see, Vegas destroys, implodes, and buries its past, just as you need to.

Well, we just killed forty-five minutes. How about we keep up the storytelling? You want something darker, huh? Read the next one. It will make the time go by.

The Hunted

The tall oak trees surrounded my view. Do you remember using a pine tree for disguise during a game of hide-and-seek as a child, or building a tree house inside an oak as a teen, or carving the name of your high school sweetheart in a white birch? I do.

As I reminisced, a cloud stole the morning sun away. I must have driven this road twenty times on my way to hunt, yet this seemed as if it were my first. A tall tree reached for the sky. It swayed in the opposite direction of the other trees. The brisk autumn wind bent it to the point of breaking. It resembled me now, my isolation amongst fellow humans, my desire to be undesirable. I felt connected to the tree. I understood its pain, understood its misplacement in the forest.

A blur entered my peripheral vision. A deer bolted in front of my speeding SUV. I hit the brakes and swerved. The tires squealed. My body bashed against the door. I heard my rifle jump from the movement. Finally, the SUV ground to a halt as the 12-point buck stopped inches from my grille.

Then, there was calmness, the moment after the storm. As I held my foot on the brake, my eyes locked with the mighty beast in front of me. I thought about plowing into him. This was the score that I craved, the score that eluded me each time I had hunted these woods, but there was an art to hunting that required the use of only one brush for the canvas—a rifle. While the buck had won this bout, I hoped he would be in my sights shortly.

"Watch it big fella," I mouthed.

Then like that, the animal kicked its hind legs and galloped into the forest. I took a deep breath, and then continued my drive, only 10 miles an hour slower this time.

I drove for another five minutes searching for the marker that I nearly passed each time. It was an orange piece of plastic that I had nailed into a tree. I placed the marker for my own direction, a breadcrumb for me to find the path into the belly of the woods. I studied each tree, looking, searching for the color orange. But I only saw the color brown.

Did someone remove my marker? I asked myself.

I pondered turning around, but just as I slowed to pull a U-turn, a piece of orange sparked the cones in my eyes.

I pulled off and killed the engine. As I opened the door, the morning's chill entered my camouflage vest and scratched my spine. It was a bittersweet feeling—the feeling that only a hunter could describe. I sifted some dirt between my fingers. I wanted to touch the skin of Mother Nature.

I filled my lungs with seclusion as I opened the rear hatch on my SUV. There she was, my Remington 7600. I grabbed a handful of .30-06 Springfield ammunition, tucked it into my vest, and then secured the gun on my back. It was a venerable weapon with a long history of buck killing. A 6-pointer was the largest hanging on my wall at home, but I hoped to double that with a kill from these isolated woods—the place where big animals were hiding.

I picked up my pack and rooted around inside. I looked for my body's ammunition—a flask. I unscrewed the cap, lifted the stainless steel, and then let a mouthful of whiskey enter my gullet. As I capped my poison and grabbed my pack, something fell onto my feet. At first, I thought it was a receipt from a stop at the adult video store, but I quickly realized it was something gravely different. I grabbed the glossy piece of paper and studied the man in the picture. He was a handsome man about forty years old with a clean shave, slick hair, and a subtle grin. He was me, one year ago. But my younger self was not the sole focus of the camera. The woman held in the man's arms was the real reason I kept the picture. She grasped a single red rose blooming at its peak in her dainty hands. The flames spewing from the fireplace behind the couple bathed her in light, glistening off her supple skin like the sun caressing tropical water. Her smile radiated; her brunette hair glistened; and her eyes allured. I studied the left hand of the man in the photograph, which gripped the young woman's waist. I envied that man, that younger version of myself. I looked down at my left hand now; dirt from the ground dirtied it. I placed the picture in my pack, locked my SUV, and then turned to embrace the breathtaking woods in front of me.

As I stepped from the gravelly macadam onto the dirt, I knew that I was leaving civilization. I pierced the wilderness to the right of the marked tree. There was a subtle yet definite path. The climb was intricate and without even realizing, the forest had swallowed me. I navigated around a large boulder and trekked up the rocky path toward my hunting spot. My brother was the only other human who knew this location— my location. I took him hunting once and only once. He scored a 10-pointer while I walked away with nothing. But today was a breathtaking morning—my morning.

Air smoked from my mouth before the cold killed it. My forty-year-old legs wobbled, but I trusted my waterproof boots to live up to their steep price tag. High-class hunting gear covered my body. Starting from inside out, I wore thermal long johns, a pair of Levi 505 regular fit jeans, a brown insulated liner, and thick camouflage pants masking me amongst my surroundings. A white size large T-shirt that said "Hoover Dam" encased my chest. A blue long sleeve work shirt and a brown sweatshirt added extra layers. Finally, a matching camouflage vest wrapped me like the largest present under the Christmas tree. The most important gear was that covering my extremities. This was the place where cold entered to chill my soul. Beyond my boots were four pairs of socks coating my feet, one more than last year after the freeze breached all three layers. A pair of thick skin-conforming gloves covered my hands, followed by a second insulated set. Then, a pair of leather-stitched camouflage gloves wrapped the outside for extra grip. Finally, a skullcap and a thermal camouflage hat covered my head. To a bird, I was invisible, but the woods knew I was there, a virus trudging deeper into its gut.

I stepped around a large stone as my eyes blurred. My boots suddenly slipped on the fine gravel. My pack dropped from my shoulder to my elbow. I tottered and reached for something...anything. Finally, my leather gloves gripped a nearby oak tree. I paused for a moment and looked down at the sharp angle I had just climbed. My breakfast from the bottle must have kicked in. I felt a twinge of sweat form on my brow, but the reinforced hat on my head quickly soaked it away.

I continued my climb as the incline finally leveled off. I stopped and turned to bask in my accomplishment. Timber consumed my view, which filtered the morning sun. Trees swayed. Birds chirped. Leaves cried. I filled my lungs with air and smiled.

There was a dense rock shaped strangely like a bench—a welcomed breadcrumb on the way to my spot. I walked around the object and continued ten more yards toward a large oak tree. I stopped on the final marker—a rock resembling a tombstone in front of the mighty oak. I stared at the living wood like a kid studying a Buckingham Palace guard. This tree was not unlike the other trees; in fact, it could have been mistaken for the others, but it was exactly ten yards behind the bench-shaped rock with a tombstone-like marker under my feet. There at chest level was a carved "X"—a signal I had made on intuition some four years ago.

I was here, but to everyone else I was nowhere. I looked straight up at the tall creature reaching for the sky, and then my eyes focused on a cloaked tree stand. Small wooden pegs led up to it, pounded in by my hands. My sense of direction had not failed me, a gift recognized at an early age. I reached into my backpack and grabbed two metal pegs. With force, I thrust them into the tree at waist level. This was the first step toward reaching the wooden pegs.

The climb was tricky as the tree seemed to growl with my climb. As I reached the top, I checked my rifle secured to my back, and then swung my body around to assume my position. The tree stand was only four feet out and three feet wide. It was a space just wide enough for one person, but I could fit two. I reached into my pack, touching the flask for only a moment, but moved on to unearth something smooth, something soft, that massaged my eyes and warmed my soul. It was the photograph of her.

I placed my partner down on my lap and carefully loaded my rifle. I only needed one shot to kill my prize, but bullets were cheap. I clutched the loaded weapon in my hand. Then, I lifted my head and filled my eyes with the wood's organs. I was far away from civilization, hidden from the naked eye, yet I felt as if I were being watched. Life flourished around me—trees shed leaves; birds flew; squirrels hopped. I sat still, dead still. While my body froze, my eyes widened, my ears opened, and my finger rested on the trigger of my rifle. I studied each twitch, each whisper, each rustle. I had to be dead, yet had to be alive within milliseconds to seize the opportunity to attack my foe. Hunting was like a showdown between bandit and sheriff—a showdown shared by exactly two.

I waited and watched every moment as my breathing rocked my body. Life seemed so simple in this position, absorbing my world through an amplifier. As my mind thought of nothing other than my visual and aural senses, a sudden and definite crack sounded in front of me. My eyes widened, grasp tightened, and heart raced as I prepared to strike the animal that had made such a prominent noise. Unexpectedly, I felt something hit my face. It was the wind of the wilderness gusting over me. Suddenly, the photograph tucked under my arm dislodged, the wind stealing it away. I reached for it like a father reaching for his darting daughter in the street, but I quickly realized that I had run out of real estate; I had exceeded my four-foot platform. I tried to go back to my spot, go back to safety, but it was too late. I fell toward the impenetrable Earth. For a split second, I felt my head smash into something. Then, I felt nothing.

I opened my eyes to a strange place. A dinner jacket covered my body. My hair was styled. My hands were clean. I saw the crackling fireplace in front of me covering me in heat. A camera sat on a tripod. Suddenly, the sweet aroma of her surrounded my nose. She was here. But then, darkness engulfed my senses. A cold chill covered my body. In a flash, I opened my eyes and saw the low angled sun over my tree stand. I had returned from the place that we went when our minds surrendered to a devastating fall.

The wind blew over me and cooled my sole. My hunting gear seemed to have failed. The sun was still low in the sky so I could have only been out for a few moments, but then I realized that the sun was not low in the east, but rather the west. It was setting—not rising! I had been unconscious for the entire day!

My brain throbbed. I shifted my shoulders and saw the painstaking rock shaped like a tombstone that had pummeled my head. I tried to sit up, but my mind screamed. Electricity shot down my right leg. It was beyond pain, a feeling without feeling. I reassessed my movements. A shape entered my field of view. I whipped my head to the side and saw the mighty beast staring at me. He was the same 12-pointer that I had met on the road, and for all I knew, he was the same animal that provoked my fall. Hunting was at the top of my mind, but the tables had been turned. I was now the bandit, hunted by the sheriff named death. The buck sniffed me, and then wandered away. He could care less about helping me, as if he knew that I would never have helped him.

I searched my right leg. I tapped and kneaded, probing for the pain, and then I found it—my knee. As I flexed my leg muscles, the pain poured.

How am I going to stand? I contemplated.

I looked nearby and found my rifle, its bent barrel victim to the fall. I clutched it, but the metal felt cold—damn cold. I needed to get up, needed to find my way back before darkness stole the light away. I grabbed one of my gloves and forced it into my mouth. I bit down as I used the rifle as a prop to stand, careful to avoid any sudden movement.

Finally, I made it up using the tree for support. I knew I had a flare in my pack. I glanced up and saw my trusty tote still sitting on the tree stand. Even though it was only ten feet away, it might as well have been ten thousand. I looked for my photograph, my partner, but all I saw were leaves. I was now alone—all alone.

The sunlight vanished from the treetops, the distant mountains consuming it. I knew I had less than thirty minutes of useable light before the void of darkness would eat all of the breadcrumbs. I used my rifle like a crutch and hobbled toward the rock-shaped bench—the first pointer. The uneven terrain made each step a painstaking task. It was as if I were reborn into a grave new world; I was a baby learning to walk. It took me fifteen seconds in the morning to get from the stone to the tree, but five minutes to go back. I was in trouble.

And just like a newborn, I turned to the only thing that worked reliably, my vocal cords.

"Help! Is anyone there! Help!"

I paused for a moment as my eardrums absorbed every bit of sound waves. All I heard were the subtle sounds of seclusion. Now, I could only use my sense of direction to continue my stumble back to my parked SUV. But I feared my senses too were a casualty to my frightening fall.

The sunset turned to twilight. I staggered toward tree after tree, taking breaks when my body quit. Night was nearly here as I kept moving, numbed to the pain. Suddenly, I saw a large boulder up ahead. My heart sang as the rock appeared to be the stone that had marked my entry point. As I neared it, my breathing picked up and my tears flowed. I caught a break on this one. As I neared the piece of Mother Nature, I realized the boulder was in the shape of something; it was in the shape of a bench. I realized that my sense of direction had failed. I was back at my starting point under the tree stand, which was now under the moon.

I realized that this was it, this was the way it was going to end, but there was something inside of me that told me to keep going, told me to keep trying. I had to get out of here. I was a cancer inside the body of the wilderness. I picked up my steps, plodding in the opposite direction—the right direction. I fought the pain as I moved.

Minutes turned into an hour, more than four times my journey in the morning. The wind froze my bones as it showered me with fallen leaves. There was no way out. I had to face that, yet I couldn't. My leg pained me, but I had to keep going—over a rock, around a tree, up an incline.

Just keep moving, I told myself, but just as I tried to ignore the reality, my crutch slipped and I fell to the Earth.

I stared at the gravel under my eyes. Just as our daily drive home becomes instinct, instinct becomes toxic when our mind loses our home. I took a deep breath and prepared to lie in my grave. I looked out at the breadth around me when something strange came into my view. It was a light—not the figurative meaning, but a real electric current passing through a thin filament. I blinked, and the light still existed. My eyes tried to adjust as my brain finally processed the image it received—a cabin.

I stood up and limped on sheer emotion toward the saving structure. It grew in my view as I cut the distance, yard by yard. Finally, I stepped beyond a tree and beheld the dominate dwelling. Wood constructed it, carefully carved and fitted to form the heart of the wilderness. It was thirty feet tall with stairs leading to its deck. I reached the base and grabbed the wooden rail. It was warm as it pumped the blood through the veins of the forest. I clumped up, step by step, finally reaching the deck.

Lights filled the inside as they stimulated my optic nerve. I crept toward the door, and there at chest level was the doorbell. I rested my index finger on the button and felt the pulse of the creature. I took a deep breath and pushed exactly one half inch. The sound of a bell scared me. Moments passed as if they were hours. As my mind raced, the door unlocked and creaked open. And there she was.

The woman was bizarrely familiar.

Is this... No, it can't be...but...

The warm glow of her face and her enticing eyes were the same as the woman in my photograph, but something didn't match. This woman had blonde hair resembling rays from the sun. My eyes traveled down her frame; a soft cotton bathrobe enveloped her hourglass figure.

"Can I help you?" the woman asked.

"Oh. Um. Yes, ma'am. I'm sorry to intrude. But I've had an accident," I stammered.

"Oh dear, what happened? Are you alright?" she said with squinted eyes.

"I think, ma'am. I just fell fifteen feet from my tree stand and hit my head. I don't know how long I was out. But I just kept walking and walking."

"I'm so sorry. Are you injured?" she asked, studying my leg.

"My ankle's twisted. But I don't think it's broken," I explained.

"Please. Come in."

"Thank you, ma'am," I replied, stepping into her world. But as I took my first step, an evil glare consumed her face.

"First of all, please don't call me ma'am. That makes me feel old," she said, changing her grimace to a grin.

She caught me off guard.

"Sorry, ma'am. I mean—"

"That's okay. I'm Tracy."

She offered me her hand. I removed my gloves, propped my rifle inside the door, and then instinctively gripped her. Her grasp was soft yet firm, warm yet cold, and inviting yet uninviting. It was different from that of the love of my life, yet it was dangerously familiar.

"The name's Jim. It's nice to meet you, Tracy," I replied with an expression my mouth hadn't formed in days—a smile.

I continued into the dwelling as its immense size absorbed me. The ceilings were vaulted and rose thirty feet into the air. What astounded me was not simply the open space, but rather the objects that breathed life into the room. More than twenty perfectly stuffed animal heads lined the off-white walls. A bison stared; an antelope glared; an elk smirked. It was like an orgy of animals—a hunter's delight.

"Wow! This is amazing. Did you hunt all these animals?" I asked as I moved toward a rug made from a lion—its head permanently frozen in a roar. The cat's fangs protruded as its look could stop anyone in his tracks.

"These are my husband's from his exotic safaris," Tracy chuckled.

I walked toward a twelve-foot-tall brown bear standing with its claws raised. I touched its fur as a shiver traveled through my spine.

"This is astounding. I bet each of these has an awesome story behind it," I said, turning back toward the most entrancing creature of them all, but she seemed uninterested, bored in fact.

"Yeah, that's my husband Jack—the *worldly* traveler. I get tired of all his trips," Tracy explained, walking into the attached kitchen. "What can I get you? Would you like something to eat or drink?"

The pain suddenly subsided. My mind had been energized, brought back into the light after the woods had cloaked it.

"Thank you. I could use some water."

"I can make you a sandwich if you'd like. And hot tea?"

"Thank you. You're way too kind," I said.

She filled a large glass with tap water and handed it to me. I guzzled it like a man heading to a bar after his wife's funeral. Who was this woman? And why was she being so kind? She was my savior, a gentle breeze through an ungentle world. I wondered whether this was her, the woman who I longed to see, to touch, to love for the past year, now somehow hidden in this cabin. I watched as she bent over to reach into the refrigerator. Her robe arched up, revealing her soft, sun-kissed legs. This had to be her, but I kept trying to convince myself that it couldn't be.

"If you have a phone, I can call for help. My brother shouldn't be too far from here. At least from where my truck is," I continued.

"That may be a problem. We're actually having trouble with our phone. It may be a while until it's back up," Tracy said as she filled a teapot with water.

"Oh really. Do you know how long?"

"I would say tomorrow at the earliest. But Jack should be back with the truck shortly. In the meantime, I'll take care of you," Tracy offered as she put the pot on the stove.

"Thank you. I don't know what I would've done if I hadn't found your place," I said lowering my head into my lap. I took a deep breath of warm air as I stared at my camouflage pants, now ripped apart. "I'm exhausted. I thought I was going to be lost in these woods forever."

I saw her shadow approach me. I lifted my head. Her eyes locked with mine. As I froze, she laid another glass of water in front of me.

"Don't worry. I'll make it all better," she muttered sending electricity through my body.

I stared at the water, too nervous to look at the beauty next to me. I felt like a beast captured in the woods.

"So Jim, how'd you end up way out here?" Tracy asked as she walked back to the stove, lowering her tail.

"Well, I usually hunt in these woods. And after I fell...I just kept walking."

"What made you fall?" she asked innocently.

I cleared my throat as the lump in my skull throbbed. "It was a strange noise right below my tree stand. I wasn't expecting it and...thump."

"Dear, that must've been awful," she said, looking at me like a wife consoling her husband.

"I don't know how long I was out. But since it's dark, I would say for at least eight hours."

Saying those words horrified me. How did I find this place? As my head pounded, Tracy wiped her hands and sauntered my way. At first, I wondered whether I was the object of her stare, but quickly she drifted past me and moved toward the lion. She reached her paw into its mouth and touched its razor sharp teeth.

"A good hunter never flinches, through thick and thin. Take this lion right here. Did you know that at full speed a lion can leap a football field in just seven strides!? Jack was down on one knee, with this beast charging full speed right at him...the most ferocious animal in the jungle was seconds from devouring him. But he stood strong, aiming ever so accurately, and took this creature out in one shot...one shot right to the brain. His crew was scared, one guy just took off running. But you see, Jack never flinched. Now that's a true sportsman."

Her story flowed through me, manipulating my brain to create images from her words.

"Wow, your husband should write a book!"

"Actually, he's written two on his hunts," she said, gesturing over her shoulder.

"I stand corrected. Who are you two? How come I never heard about your place from my taxidermist?" I asked.

But before she could answer, a whistle pierced my ears. It sounded like a cry of death, a noise that entered my ears and stabbed my brain. I thought it was the sound of reality trying to wake me from a dream, but as I turned my head, I realized it was the teapot. I watched Tracy hustle to the whistle. Who was this woman? And more importantly, who was her husband? Perhaps, I was this man and this was my home. I wondered whether this was some alternate reality, a time and a place that paralleled my existence. Perhaps, this would have been my life had the love of my life not passed away.

"What kind of tea would you like?" Tracy asked as she rummaged through the cupboard. "I have green tea, black tea, and some peppermint tea."

Her simple query caught me off guard. Here I was thinking about alternate worlds but all she wanted to know was the type of tea I liked.

"Green tea would be fine," I guessed.

I studied her movements as if I were hunting. She removed a bag from a tin in the cupboard, placed it into a cup, and then doused it with the scalding water. I watched as the string from the tea bag draped over the side of the cup. Steam swirled around killing the helpless tea leaves. Then, she brought me the concoction with one hand and the meaty sandwich with the other.

"Thank you," I mechanically replied as the smell of the blasted leaves entered my nose and aroused my senses. I stared at the drowning tea bag.

"Good choice. I drink a lot of green tea. It's very high in antioxidants. Helps me keep my girlish figure," Tracy purred.

I lifted my head as Tracy's words entered my mind and traveled throughout my body. She opened her bathrobe revealing a set of black lingerie. I couldn't look, yet I couldn't look away. The lace contoured her plump breasts as the warm light bounced off the soft skin of her belly. My wandering eyes rested on the black panties that caged the cabin's most ferocious beast.

"Do you find me attractive, Jim?" she asked so softly that I could barely hear her, yet I heard her louder than anything. She shook her hips, stopping my heart. I was speechless, tangled in her slippery web.

"Well, ma'am, yes, uh, I do," I stumbled.

"Good, because Jack works a lot and takes these long safaris, which can make a girl go crazy."

I was overwhelmed. Her words roused my libido, but four letters that emitted from her vocal cords frightened me beyond the pleasures that her bite would offer—the four letters that spelled her husband's name. I envisioned a beefy man, above six feet tall, with more powerful rifles and even denser camouflage than I had. For all I knew, he was cloaked in the house, waiting, watching to see if I would make a move on his wife. I needed to break free from her trance so I stared at man's second need for survival—food.

"Uh, do you have any pickles?" I asked, eyeing my sandwich.

"Yeah, you're right. Jack should be home shortly," she reasoned. "I think I have pickles."

And then like that, she relinquished her grip and focused her sights on pickled cucumbers. I took a sip of the brew; it scorched my mouth and burned my throat. Its temperature was just right as it warmed my frozen soul.

"They're sweet pickles. Is that okay?" she asked.

"Argh! Sweet!?" I said, detesting the rotten flavor.

"They're Jack's favorite," Tracy replied.

I bit my lip as I looked at the ham, salami, and Swiss cheese held in place by two slices of whole wheat bread. I needed a pickle not because of its taste, but because it reminded me of a lunch back home; it reminded me of sanity.

"Well...I'm a dill fan, but ya gotta have a pickle with a sandwich," I said as she handed me the jar. "Thank you."

"If you say *thank you* one more time, I'm going to have to shoot you," she said.

I looked at her tempting eyes, searching for an answer to this mysterious woman. Her kindness cradled me, but her sarcasm terrified me. I remembered hunting with my grandfather thirty years ago, sitting for hours with his wisdom. And one frequent saying that he always offered was that many a truth was said in jest. I wished I were with him now, protected by his rifle, but I was far, far away from him. My only companion now was a sandwich. I raised it to my mouth and took a bite. I was beyond hungry, my taste buds numbed to the lack of nourishment. But as the food entered my mouth, I received a blast of energy.

"I'll let you eat. I'll be right back. I'm going to change," Tracy said as she snaked past me, leaving me alone.

I felt as if I were back home, eating lunch after one of my hunts. I took a bite of the pickle, paused as my taste buds deliberated, and then swallowed it. It wasn't as bad as I had expected. As I chomped on my meal, my eyes roamed around the room looking for something, anything that would settle my curious mind about this bizarre cabin. The refrigerator lacked magnetized pictures. The drapes were pattern-less. The coffee mugs on the counter were generic. In front of me were some hunting magazines. I flipped through them as a picture caught my eye on the cover of one of them. It was Tracy, decorated by camouflage, holding a rifle, and kneeling next to a 12-point buck. She had a brazen look about her, the look of a hunter after her kill.

Why is she on the cover of this magazine? I mulled in my mind.

I thought Jack was the hunter. This image only added to the eeriness surrounding me. I studied the monstrous buck on the cover and knew that I had to find it on the wall. I took the last bite of my sandwich, grabbed my green tea, and then lurched into the living room to find the head.

The room was like a morgue. The crackling fire filled the vast space. I stepped around the lion rug, careful to avoid its jaws. The bear stood above me. I moved toward the center of the room, cautious of the bear's grasp. I looked at the beasts on the wall, as I felt their eyes burning into me. I knew they saw me, all of them waiting for my guard to drop. I didn't remember why I had come in here. I took another drink of my tea, now cool enough to gulp. A bison on the wall captivated me. It seemed alive, as if it were about to move at any moment. I gravitated toward it and studied the fiend. Its long furry snout appeared moist as if the creature were still breathing.

"That was from the Yukon," Tracy said, the echo of her voice startling my oversensitive nerves.

I turned to her voice. My eyes received the striking image of the venomous vixen covered by a black night slip. The radiating black silk accentuated her deadly curves as yet again she held me in her grasp.

"Don't be alarmed," she purred as her swirling scent tickled my nose. "The bison doesn't bite, at least not anymore."

Tracy slinked toward the couch as her hips mesmerized me. They swayed perfectly like a ticking clock. She sat down and gestured for me to join her. Acting on instinct, I followed her lead on the loveseat. I set my teacup down on an end table and looked at her as I had looked at the love of my life.

"Can I be honest with you on something?" I asked.

"Oh. You have a secret. Do tell!"

"Well, Tracy. You actually have a striking resemblance to my wife," I finally revealed.

"You're married?"

I held my head down as her question pummeled me like that rock.

"I was. She died in a car accident. About a year ago. Actually, I think it's a year to the day."

"Aw... I'm so sorry to hear that," she said with a genuine look of compassion.

I suddenly felt protected. I carried this weight around me since my wife had passed away. She was my sweetheart, my sunshine during a dark day, my breath of fresh air in a stuffy room. She left me without saying good-bye, and I think about her every moment of my life, now more than ever.

"Yeah, she was a great woman. I think about her every day," I said.

"Do you get out much?"

"Ha, well if going out in the woods counts, but—"

"Are you warm enough? I feel like adding another log to the fire," she interjected.

"Oh, I'm okay."

Unexpectedly, she changed from sympathetic to apathetic. Tracy sprang from her seat and pounced on the fireplace.

"No, I want to. We need to keep you warmed up…" she said without turning, but then she twisted her head and stared at me. "…if you want to live."

Her words perforated my ears. At first, I wondered how her tone could change so quickly, but her attack was covert. I stood up and tried to take cover, but as soon as my body rose, the room began to spin. I lifted my hand to my brow as my breathing intensified. I had to escape from her grasp, but something was seriously wrong.

"Ugh. I…I don't feel right," I exhaled.

I glanced at the teacup, and then back at my predator. She held a piece of wood in her hand. I tried to move, but I couldn't. I tried to think, but my mind stopped. Light faded, and then I saw darkness.

I suddenly sprang awake at the sight of fire. I looked at the blazing fireplace, and then turned to look for Tracy, but as I did I saw a much smaller living room—my living room. The woman who approached me had killer curves and an alluring smile, but her hair was not blonde; it was brown. It was her, my wife. I didn't know what to do, yet I knew exactly what do. I reached to the side and grabbed a single red rose from a vase. I handed it to my princess as she sat down. Then, I jumped to set the self-timer on the awaiting camera. As the light flashed red, I returned to my wife's side and scooped her waist, her succulent scent invigorating me. She was alive here next to me. Her warmness flowed through my hand and to my heart. I felt the blood pumping in her veins giving her and myself life. This was real, yet it couldn't be. I prepared for the camera to flash, but I heard a voice whisper.

"Wake up."

I turned to my princess, but she remained motionless.

"Wake up."

A blinding white light burst from the camera. I felt like a newborn being born into the world. Suddenly, a woman's face came into focus. It was my wife, but as the white light dissipated, her hair was the wrong color—blonde.

"Wake up. Wake up," Tracy instructed.

My mind finally returned, but the line blurred between dream and reality. Perhaps, this too was all a dream.

"What... What happened?" I stumbled, finding myself lying on Tracy's couch surrounded by dead heads.

She still wore the black night slip, but I no longer craved her; I detested her. She was sitting on the end of the couch with a knife in her hand slicing a deep red apple. I was terrified, yet I was glad that a piece of fruit was occupying her and not a piece of me.

"You were out for almost an hour," Tracy said without taking her eyes away from her task. Her voice was deeper, rawer as she sliced the apple into pieces. "Maybe it was the sweet pickle," she joked.

"Ugh...my head," I exhaled, my skull throbbing like an open wound. "What were you saying before?"

"Well, Jack's back. He's upstairs showering," Tracy muttered without removing her stare from the fruit.

"Oh. Did he ask about me?" I asked, widening my eyes.

"I told him about your accident. He wants to help, but would rather you stay awhile to tell you about some of his safari stories."

Her words were bittersweet. Sweet in that I had a potential escape from this black widow through her husband, but bitter in that he could be the worse half of the marriage.

"Thank you. But I should get going. I would appreciate if he could just run me to town," I tactfully replied. "By the way, if you could please write down your address and number. I want to send you something for your troubles," I lied.

"Don't be silly. You're our guest. Jack wants you to stay...*I* want you to stay."

"No, that would be—"

"You're staying!" she barked.

I froze as she held me in her eyes. She dropped the apple and clutched the knife. Its sterling silver reflected the inferno spewing from the fireplace. She had lost interest in the fruit, which terrified me. I didn't know whether I should run, but I couldn't count on my beaten body to respond. I too had to rely on stealth; I needed to become a cunning cat.

Tracy moved toward the kitchen, her intentions unknown. I waited until she removed me from her focus, and then I rose slowly. I realized I needed protection against this ravenous beast. I needed my rifle, busted or not, as its hard-encased metal would surely take down this creature. But as I glanced toward the door only ten feet away, the rifle had vanished from the spot where I had propped it.

"Here, let me give you my address and number," Tracy offered as she wrote on a red notepad.

I watched her movements as if I were hunting from my tree stand. She folded the paper and handed it to me, but as my fingers grazed hers, a blast of sound erupted behind her; it was the telephone.

"Hey, I thought you said the phone didn't work?" I said.

"It just came back up," Tracy said, answering it.

I trembled in fear. This woman, in fact, this whole cabin was full of lies.

"Hello?" Tracy spoke into the phone.

Now was my chance. I whipped around and bolted toward the door. I grabbed the cold doorknob and twisted, but it didn't budge. I tried to unlock it, but every turn yielded the same result. I saw three intricate deadbolts protecting an intruder from entering, or in this case, a lost traveler from exiting.

"I have an unexpected visitor," Tracy said into the phone as she glared at me.

There was no way out. I thought of my grandfather again and his proverbs. I remembered him saying that if there was no way out, look for a deeper way in. My only hope now was the man of the house, a man who I hoped was sane and could keep his wife in check, a man who was now upstairs. I darted through the living room, and through the pain, to the long stairway. It traversed the side of the monstrous room and provided a view from some fifteen feet above. At the top, there were three doors, two of which were closed, but as I stopped for a moment to try to listen beyond my pounding heart, I heard the shower faintly from within the only open room.

I entered the bedroom. The sound of the running water intensified with each step toward the attached bathroom. A king-size bed stood in the center of the open space. There were gun racks housing rifles like wine in an aristocrat's cellar. Bones and animal tusks accented the firepower.

Where are the windows? I asked myself.

The smell of mothballs hit my nose. The light from the attached bathroom shined into the room, cutting it, half in light and half in shadow.

"Jack? Excuse me, sir. I was wondering if I could ask for a ride?...Jack?"

The shower seemed to grow in intensity. There was no turning back now. I was too far into the hole. I tiptoed toward the bathroom, my eyes wide and white. I didn't want to disturb the man, yet I had no choice. I stepped off the carpet and into the tiled bathroom. The blinding fluorescent lights punched my pupils. White surrounded me with the mist of water vapor hanging in the room.

"Jack?" I murmured, but the running water only mocked me.

I minced toward the opaque curtain. My breathing picked up; my heart pounded. This was it. I raised my hand. Then in one swoop, I flung open the curtain.

An empty shower stared back, the water running. There was no burly man named Jack before me. My eyes followed the stream down toward the drain as the color of clear water changed to rusty red. There were a half dozen heavily used bear traps soaking. Bone and skin fragments covered the rusted metal and backed up the water in the tub. The bloody water was near the top. As I stared in utter fear, the water trickled over the white porcelain, and then poured into the bathroom.

I jumped away from the mess. Near the toilet, there was a display stand with framed pictures. I grabbed the top one as my eyes beheld the woman of the house, Tracy, decorated in superior hunting gear. She kneeled next to the killed lion in the African jungle, a powerful rifle in her hand. Written below was "Tracy with her accurate rifle 'Jack' during her lion hunt."

The horrific truth revealed itself. Jack was her man, but he was not flesh and bones; he was metal and screws. I threw the picture down. It smashed on the cold, hard tile. I paused, contemplating my next move. I could not think. I was lost in the bowels of the ominous cabin. I looked at myself in the bathroom mirror and saw the red paper that Tracy had given me. I removed it from my vest and unfolded it. I prepared to read her telephone number and address—useless information at this point—but what I saw sent a shudder throughout my body. It read, "You're never leaving and if you do I will find you…"

I tore up the paper and threw it into the air. It rained over me as if from an angry sky. I stopped breathing as I studied the man in the mirror. He was white as a ghost and scrapes and bruises painted his face. He was a man I did not recognize, and for this man, he had the hardest fight of his life in front of him.

"Oh my God," I mumbled, searching for strength.

Pain still throbbed through my bones, but I had to flee. There was only one way out now and that was the front door. I needed claws, fangs, or sheer muscle to brute force my way out, but I had none of those. The rusty bear traps were worthless. The murky water reached my boots, as I knew time was running out. I hurled bottles of soap and toothpaste aside on the counter; I found nothing useful. I flung open the medicine cabinet. I tossed the first shelf. A bottle of mouthwash detonated. Pills spilled over the counter. I grabbed a nail file, but it couldn't pierce a lion's hide. I found a pair of scissors. I wielded them as I would a machete. These were pitiful, but they were the best I could do. I slammed the medicine cabinet shut. The glass cracked, slicing the man in the mirror in half.

I stepped through the muddy water as it penetrated my boots. It was warm, but that was because I was cold. I walked through the bedroom holding the scissors. As my body trembled, I saw the door to the hallway.

The air in the hallway was cool as it hit the sweat on my brow. I made it to the banister. I peered over. I saw the black fur of the bison, the brown bear, and the sandy lion, but I didn't see the color blonde. My attacker was not in view. I crept down each step, the carpet muffling my shoes. The sound of the overflowing tub was a distant hum.

I made it to the bottom of the stairs. I peered around the corner looking for any sign of movement. I saw a shadow looming. I tried to follow it, my sweaty hands clasping the scissors. A crack sounded. I jumped. The scissors fell. As my body screamed, I realized the noise was the cry of a log incinerated by the fire. The shadow was from the grizzly bear.

I saw the door only twenty feet away. I left the scissors lie and grabbed a piece of firewood nearby. I made my break for the door, ready to shatter the glass to escape. I pushed through the pain, shaving the distance between me and safety.

As I passed the kitchen, a flicker entered the corner of my eye. The object caused me to stop cold. It was a can of some sort, which I gravitated toward, but the object resting on top opened my eyes. It was a single red rose. My mind shifted to my wife. I held the rose and sniffed its beauty...hypnotized. Then, I looked at the can, which sat next to my teacup. I read its label—"Rat Poison."

My body and my mind convulsed. I could feel the poison running through my arteries. A shadow shifted in front of me. I looked up. It was the image of beauty, and the image of death. It was Tracy holding my rifle and charging at me like a lion. She grunted as I twisted to the side, but her drive was too strong. She whacked me on the head. My body flew back, my eyes swirling in my head. I soared toward the door. My eyes saw it, but my body did not. I crashed through the living room window. I toppled down the stairs, my head bashing against each wooden step. All I saw were the floodlights, and I knew I had to run away from them, away from danger. I didn't know where my aggressor was, but I had to keep moving as long as I could. I bobbled forward faster and faster when suddenly the ground gave way to a steep incline. I tumbled head first down the rocky slant past trees and boulders. Each turn pounded my body. Then, light became black as my body bashed into something impenetrable.

I was in a void, a moment where nothing existed. It was a feeling without feeling, a dream without dreaming. Suddenly, the black became intense light. I was in the middle of a blaze. I turned trying to determine my location and saw a red sedan spewing fire. I knew now exactly where I was. I moved through the inferno to the driver's side door and saw the woman trapped inside, the woman whom I could never forget—my wife.

As I watched her demise, I heard a bird chirping. The noise increased as I looked up at the sky. The sun was out. Then, it all became clear. I left my moment of emptiness and returned to the world. I was on the ground, my head resting on the rock that had induced my blackout. I realized that Tracy had not killed me. She had left me in the wilderness. I looked toward the location of her cabin, but the hill that I had plummeted down masked it. I was given a second chance.

As my mind raced, I heard the sound of something walking. I realized I was out in the open, prey for a hungry beast. I feared it was Tracy, waiting until the sunrise to finish me off and add my head to her wall. I couldn't move. My body was too badly beaten. I had to accept my fate. I hoped my passing would be quick and painless. I moved my head as the image of the being came into view; it was a high-class hunter. The man stopped at my sight.

"Hello! Are you okay?" the hunter yelled, running my way.

I breathed a sigh of relief. The man was young, about twenty-five, and he was my savior.

"Sir, are you alright? Can you hear me?" the man asked, offering me his hand. "Are you okay?"

"Ugh. What happened? Where is she?" I finally said.

"Sir, I think you hit your head. Can you stand?" he asked.

"I think so," I replied as he helped me.

My head throbbed in pain, but I felt protected by the man's grasp.

"Where is she?" I asked.

"What?"

"The woman? Where is she?"

"It looks like you hit your head, sir," the hunter said as he gestured up.

I followed his gaze and saw something troubling. It was my tree stand. I couldn't believe it. Was the cabin this close to my tree stand? How did I fall under it?

"Her cabin is just up there," I said.

"Sir, there is nothing for miles and miles around here. You hit your head from falling from your tree stand. The mind can play tricks on you," he explained as he helped me hobble away.

It was impossible. The experience was so real. I was there. She was with me. I knew it, yet I couldn't be certain. Perhaps, it was all a dream.

I remained speechless as we walked out of the woods. I couldn't think anymore. I needed to get back to civilization. As we moved together through the brush, the wind blew a piece of paper caught in my jacket's zipper. At first, I thought it was the picture of my wife, accompanying me this whole time, but it wasn't a photograph; it was a torn piece of paper the color of deep red.

"Wait," I told my savior.

I stopped it from blowing away with my boot. It was a piece from the note that I had read in the cabin's bathroom. The small two inch by two inch colored paper explained everything. As I read the phrase aloud, my heart stopped—"I will find you..."

Our minds are powerful things. In Vegas, the mind can be your worst enemy. That was one of my favorite stories.

Do you want to try selling some T-shirts? Okay. Just grab a shirt and give them a line. Here, let me show you. This Hoover Dam black looks good.

Souvenir T-shirts! Three for ten! Do you want one, ma'am? How about you, sir? Get some for your family. You like those three? Great. I'll ring you up over here.

See, now that wasn't hard. That guy is kinda cute. He actually reminds me of the guy in the next story.

The Chef

A hotel room sits dormant. Suddenly, the door opens as a man stands at the doorway, silhouetted by light from the hall. He enters like a cold breeze, flips the light switch, and then shuts the door. The man's slicked-back hair reaches for the collar of a black pinstriped suit. He looks to be about thirty-five, but then again, he could be older. The man is smooth yet rough, visibly striking yet invisibly menacing. He looks as if he could play James Bond, but at a second look, he could play his villain. The man possesses a peculiar feature that stands out yet is hidden. He has the power to stop someone cold, stimulating him or her to deduce that odd quality, just as he did a mother of four in the elevator.

The man carries a large duffel bag, the kind that a sporting goods store has to special order. He sets the bag on the queen-size bed, and then fixes his collar. He glides around the room so softly that a blind man would miss him. The man looks inside the bathroom. Fresh towels, complimentary toiletries, and a spotless mirror fill his gaze.

The man shifts to the side of the room. He grazes the top of a wooden chair, which is part of a five-piece dining room set. Then, he beholds the small kitchenette. A stainless-steel refrigerator shines. A microwave glistens. A faucet in the sink begs to be turned on. The man focuses on the item next to them—a gas stove. He walks to it, and then caresses its polished metal, running his fingers around a burner. Then, he turns the knob. He waits for the fire, but the stove appears lifeless. He twists another knob, but the stove only mocks him.

The man storms to the phone next to the bed and dials the operator.

"Hi, this is the front desk. How may I help you?" a female voice answers.

"I just checked into room three twenty one. There seems to be a problem," the man says as he folds a piece of paper on the nightstand to amuse himself.

"Oh, Mister Divine. What can I do to fix this problem?" the female asks.

"Well, you gave me a room without a working stove. Are you trying to sabotage me?"

"I'm terribly sorry, sir. Let me see what I can do for you," the woman consoles. "Unfortunately, all our rooms are filled tonight. How about a complimentary buffet or show ticket?"

"Buffet? You must be joking. Listen to me. This is unacceptable!" the man barks.

"I will send a repairman up right away."

"Make it snappy. I need to practice my special dish so I'm prepared tomorrow," he says.

"Certainly, sir. I apologize for the inconvenience," the woman says.

The man hangs up the phone and takes a deep breath. He lets it out slowly, trying to calm his nerves. The man moves to his bag. He unpacks it on top of the bed, carefully laying everything on the sheet. He removes a white chef uniform and a matching hat. Then, he unearths a satchel of cooking supplies and a clear plastic bag filled with spices. Next, he exposes a wine bottle protected by a hard case. The man holds it in his hand as if his fingers want a taste. Finally, he removes thick plastic sheets folded neatly.

And then, black becomes white as a conversion occurs in the confined hotel room. The man's hands button up the white chef jacket. He positions the white hat perfectly on his head. Oregano, Parsley, Turmeric, Basil, and Thyme bottles line up on the side kitchenette counter. The man puts the wine on ice. A spatula slides from the satchel. The man removes a butcher knife as it sparkles under the bright lights.

An image appears in the mirror next to the bed. Mirrors judge everything equally, but this particular one reflects something that has no equal. Right there in the room a transformation has taken place—the man has become the chef.

The chef admires his outfit. He straightens his hat and adjusts his collar. As he stares, a knock pounds on the door. The chef opens it; a repairperson greets him. The chef beholds not an overweight slob with a gut hanging over his belt, but rather a fetching woman fitted with a pressed work suit. "Stacy" is proudly displayed on her name badge. She does not fit the mold of a typical hotel worker, but then again, this is not a typical hotel.

"Hello, sir. There's a problem with your stove?" the repairwoman asks.

"A big problem," the chef says.

"I know why you're here," she replies glancing at his uniform. "Hmm. I thought we inspected all the stoves for the event."

"Well, you missed mine."

The chef invites her in as she scurries to perform her job, not noticing him turn the deadbolt. He moves lightly as she moves quickly. The chef eyes her utility belt fitted with a walkie-talkie. He contemplates her measurements, figuring her trim waist to be just over two feet.

"A repairwoman? It's been a long time since I've had a woman," the chef says.

"It's tough work, but hey, I need the money," Stacy says, her cheeks blushing.

She replies to the awkwardness by scuttling to the stove. While she bends to work, the chef maintains his focus on her figure. That odd quality surfaces as he ogles her; it's in his beady eyes.

"Looks like your pilot's out. Good thing there's a safety switch on these models to prevent a gas leak," the repairwoman explains from the ground.

She pulls out a stick lighter from her belt and lights the pilot—a task she knows all too well from the past three days preparing for the hotel's big event. Stacy stands up and tries the burner. This time the stove ignites. The chef smiles.

"You're all set," she says without making eye contact.

"Perfect," he replies shifting his stare from the stove to the woman.

She removes the walkie-talkie.

"This is Stacy. The stove in room three twenty one is fixed. Pilot was out," she radios.

"Roger that. Can you check five sixteen? Bathroom light is burned out," the burly voice of her boss replies.

"I haven't taken my dinner break yet," Stacy says.

"You can eat later. There's work to do."

"Roger. I'm on my way," she says, rolling her eyes.

The repairwoman notices the spices on the table, culinary utensils, and cooking pot. She is ready to leave, but her stomach growls.

"So, what are you cooking tonight?" she asks.

The chef removes his focus from Stacy. He palms his butcher knife and buffs it with a cloth.

"A plump and juicy steak," he replies.

"But where's the meat?" she chuckles.

Stacy's laugh echoes in the confined space. She looks at the chef, hoping to see a lighthearted reply, but all he does is stare at her with menacing eyes.

"I've actually only consumed the male *Homo sapiens*. A female will be a very special treat," the chef says, staring at her breasts.

She squints her eyes in confusion. Working in a transient hotel provides her with a fair share of odd guests; this one is the oddest.

"Uh, I'm just going to go now," she says, moving to the door.

Stacy sees the emergency exit information plastered on the hotel room door. She is only steps away from the exit, steps away from freedom. She reaches for the knob, but a long dagger embeds into the wood of the door. She stops cold.

"You forgot your tip," the chef says.

Stacy doesn't look back. She grabs the handle, but another knife slashes her hand. She shrieks as her walkie-talkie falls from her grasp. She glances at it, but sees the chef charging toward her. She chooses to flee into the only other location—the bathroom.

Stacy dives into the room, slams the door, and then twists the lock. Darkness surrounds her as the door rattles. She runs to the back wall. Tears flow down her face as she realizes that she is now safe, but also, she realizes that she is now trapped. Through the darkness, she watches the light trickle in from below the door, broken by the shoes of her attacker. Her breathing rocks her body; her heart pounds. She remains still, frozen like ice. Then, she sees her stalker leave.

Stacy reaches for the switch, filling the space with light. She stares at her frizzled brown hair drenched by her tears. The pain finally sets in as her adrenaline subsides. She looks at her hand. Blood drips onto the tiled floor. Stacy grabs a towel and wraps it around her open wound, which throbs with each beat of her heart.

"Stacy, can you stop by five eleven first? Looks like a clogged toilet," faintly seeps through the bathroom door from the walkie-talkie.

Stacy presses her ear against the door.

In the room, the chef coasts to the device. He studies it. The rubber call button intrigues him.

"Stacy? Are you there?" the walkie-talkie vibrates through the chef's masculine hand.

Her boss' voice sends electricity through her beaten body.

"They're going to come looking for me. You better let me go," Stacy says through the door.

"They won't care about a measly little repairwoman," the chef replies.

"Stacy? Why aren't you answering!?" the walkie-talkie expels.

The chef turns off the device.

Inside the bathroom, Stacy searches for something...anything. She flings the complimentary soap to the ground. A grate on the ceiling catches her attention. She stands on the toilet and yells into it.

"Help! Anyone! Help!"

There is a subtle knock at the door. Stacy wavers, and then topples toward the unyielding tile. Her ankle twists. She screams.

"There's only one way out, my dear. It should only hurt for a moment," the chef's voice oscillates through the door.

Stacy grabs the shower curtain. She pulls herself halfway up. But the curtain snaps and her body bashes against the tub. Her wound splits. Blood gushes on the floor.

Three knocks emit through the door. Stacy groans. She opens the drawer under the sink. Inside, she pulls out a freestanding placard that says, "We hope you have an enjoyable stay – Management." She throws it against the door. Stacy does her best to stand. She looks at the mirror, and then clutches a towel. She wraps her uncut hand, and then punches the mirror.

The reflecting glass cracks, as does her skin. She increases her intensity. Blood saturates the towel. She cries as her brain squeals. She dislodges a large piece of broken glass from the mirror.

Stacy stares at the looming door. She tries to silence her snivels. An eerie silence consumes her. Suddenly, she hears a toilet flush upstairs. She thinks about the normalcy above her, the guest in room 421 preparing for sleep. But she knows that she is not in room 421, she is stuck in the confines of the room equivalent to hell.

Stacy sneaks to the door. She puts her ear against the cool oak. Then, she listens for a sound. Stillness replies. She places her bloody hand on the lock, and then twists it through the pain. While Stacy has opened thousands of bathroom doors during her year on the job, she opens the bathroom door in room 321 the slowest.

The abandoned room welcomes her. She sees the closed door to the hall, the door to freedom. Stacy slithers toward it, her twisted ankle pulsating. Her utility boots muffle on the soft carpet. Two steps to safety, something catches her eyes. She sees thick plastic covering the bed. Suddenly, a shadow moves.

The chef grabs Stacy like a piece of meat. The shard of glass drops to the ground. Stacy squirms. A knock sounds at the door, only six feet away. Stacy tries to yell, but the chef raises a knife to her neck. She feels the cold blade against her throat. Stacy freezes.

The chef slides toward the knock with the repairwoman on his side. He opens the door only a crack as he hides his victim behind the stout piece of wood. Stacy's burly boss locks eyes with the chef.

"Sorry to bother you, sir. Was there a repairwoman here before?" the boss asks.

The chef glances at the 100 pounds of meat in his hand. She wriggles. The chef tightens his grip.

"She stormed out of here. Said she was quitting the job because of not getting a break," the chef lies.

"Uh… Okay. Hmm. Well, I'm sorry to have bothered you, sir," the boss says.

While he is only two feet from his employee, two feet that usually separates him from a talk with a staff member, one inch of strong wood divides these twenty-four inches.

The chef closes the door and clicks the deadbolt sealing him and his victim inside the room. Stacy tries to duck. She breaks free for a second, but the chef tosses her on the bed.

"You're a sick man. What are you doing?" Stacy pleads as she sits up facing her predator.

"All this work has made me very hungry," the chef says, towering over her with a butcher knife.

Stacy has a moment to scream, but then the chef uncoils his sculpted bicep on his right arm and slices her flesh. She drops onto the plastic. Blood splatters on the headboard. Another chop, and then another. The chef grunts with each cleave.

Moments later, a slab of finely cut meat plops on the frying pan. It sizzles. The chef sprinkles some parsley and oregano on the cooking meat. Then, he sets a steak knife and fork next to a large glistening plate. After that, deep red wine pours into a glass. He dips his finger into it, testing its temperature. As the chef works like an artist painting his masterpiece, the meat cooks until the juices and tenderness align. He spears it and sits the superbly cooked meat on the dish.

The chef removes his hat and uniform, changing from meat preparer to meat consumer. He sits at the side table and swirls his wine glass, sipping the red concoction. Then, he takes the steak knife and cuts a sliver of meat.

Suddenly, a phone rings. The man shakes his head and stands to answer the phone.

"Yes?" he says.

"Hello, sir. This is the front desk again. I wanted to ensure your problem has been rectified," the familiar voice asks.

"Ah. Yes. A nice young lady took care of it."

"Very well. Well good luck tomorrow, Mister Divine. Do you know what you're going to be cooking for the competition?"

"Yes, a very special meat."

"Excellent. Well, I'm one of the judges. I can't wait to taste it."

He looks at the repairwoman's dead body enveloped in plastic. A gory gash exposes the raw flesh under her shoulder and breast. The man hangs up the phone and moves back toward his awaiting meal. He sits down and stabs the carved meat with his fork. Then, he raises it to his salivating mouth and slides it inside. The man inhales and chews, his eyes rolling back.

Through the plastic, a look of horror covers the repairwoman's departed face.

I read that story every time I meet a guy with that quality you just can't place, which is more times than a heart breaks in this city.

The view is nice from here. I like the Monte Carlo across the street. It is one of those casinos that I never get to. The Strip is not that big if you think about it. Sure, walking takes you hours, but you can drive it in twenty minutes. Nevada is such a strange place. I don't know why people keep moving here.

Well, only one more hour of this hell. I have to curb my hunger. That last story made my mouth water. That guy over there looks tasty. Haha. Keep an eye out for customers while you check out the next story. I'll be back.

The Courier

A deserted road seemed to lead into the cloudless blue sky. The sun penetrated the barren desert. The only thing moving was the radiating heat. Old cars that once provided transportation were now scorched metal shells. The word "Grocery" was barely visible on the side of a billboard, victim to the sweltering heat. The place was as lifeless as a dying planet consumed by the living sun. Suddenly, something black shifted over the crest.

Wheels of a sport bike spun on the macadam as the engine hummed. Flawless black leather boots rested on the pegs. Leather pants conformed to the biker's skin. A black jacket enveloped the rider. An opaque helmet concealed the biker's identity. A black duffel bag was anchored to the back with bungee ties. It was hard to distinguish where the biker stopped and the bike started, but it appeared that this creature had one goal, one title—courier.

Mountains blurred by the rocket traveling at triple digit speeds. It maintained perfect accuracy on the center of the road like a bullet blasted from a gun. Up ahead, the gutted car obstructed the bike's path. The courier kept the throttle pegged. The bike swerved, blew by the car, and then returned to the center of the road. The beaten billboard didn't distract the bike as it sped by. Hidden on the other side was a police car with blacked-out windows. The car appeared abandoned at first, but as soon as the missile whizzed past, the lights and siren screamed alive.

The car squealed its tires as it pulled out. The V8 engine devoured the dry desert air. Its speed increased with each second, but the bike was now just a speck of black.

The courier glanced into the side view mirror, as the enraged machine seemed to be no match. The bike pulled full throttle ahead. But just as the courier appeared unstoppable, a white unmarked police truck stared eye-to-eye with the speeding bike.

A light swirled on the truck's roof as its siren blared. Black tint consumed its windows. The truck sustained its drive into the direct path of the speeding bike. The courier had no way out. The distance between the bike and the truck narrowed.

The courier kept the engine at full throttle. The truck opened its jaws. In a flash, the bike swerved inches from the truck's bite. The force was too much as the courier flew into the air and toppled over and over on the desert ground. The black leather scraped the cracked ground. The bike slid to a halt as the duffel bag hurled into the air. Finally, the courier stopped.

Both police vehicles followed the downed bike. Their sirens died as the sound of silence erupted. Seconds passed which seemed like hours as stillness once again consumed the desert. Then, the doors burst open from the vehicles. Three men poured out, masked by colored bandanas. Dust caked on their sunburned skin as only their beady eyes showed. The one driving the sedan was as skinny as a rake and wore blue. From the passenger side of the car, a longhaired goon covered by the color red stepped out like a self-made captain after pulling the shortest straw. The overzealous husky man in yellow ran from the driver's seat of the truck. The men looked tough, yet vulnerable—tough like bullies in junior high, but vulnerable when they became freshmen.

"You dumb ass. I told you not to hit 'em. Just get 'em to pull over," Red barked at Yellow.

"Sorry, boss. This one didn't wanna stop," Yellow replied.

"Blue, you check his pockets. And Yellow, you search the bike," Red continued.

Blue and Yellow jumped into action. Their metallic boots kicked up sand as they entered the desert. Blue neared the immobile courier. He examined the black leather now covered with sand.

"He don't have no pockets, boss," Blue yelled.

"Damn it! These varmints come into our territory uninvited, and they don't have nothin' to pay our toll."

"Wait, I think there's somethin' here," Yellow exclaimed as he saw the duffel bag.

"What is it?" Red shouted.

Yellow grabbed the bag and cleaned off the grit. It was made of a thick, almost metallic, material that barely bent. As Yellow flipped it over, a potent keyed lock mocked him.

"There's a lock on this here bag. There has to be somethin' of value inside," Yellow exclaimed as he brought the bag back to Red.

"What do you think it is, boss?" Blue asked.

"Give it here, let me look!" Red roared as he snatched it. "Hmm, get the tin snips from the car."

"I bet it's a million bucks. We hit it rich!" Blue exclaimed, running to the police cruiser.

"It's packs of somethin'. It has to be money. And there's a bunch of it," Red said, feeling the bag.

"Yee-haw!" Yellow howled.

Blue returned with a pair of flimsy snips. Red grabbed them, and then tried to cut. The tool failed. He tried another angle, but the snips were useless.

"Damn it! What the hell is this shit made of? I've never seen nothin' like it," Red said.

"Can I try, boss?" Yellow asked.

"No! Me and Blue are taking this back to the Kremlin. You grab what you can off the bike," Red commanded.

"Why do I always have to do the grunt work?"

"Because I'm in charge! And plus you're the one that almost killed him."

And then like that, Red and Blue jumped into the cruiser and sped away chirping the underinflated tires on the macadam. Yellow listened to the V8 feast on the desert air.

"Make Yellow do it. Hey Yellow, go pick up that there cactus for us," Yellow mocked.

He glanced at the motionless courier baking under the sun. Yellow shook his head and moped toward the downed bike. He kneeled to check the powerful machine. Its lines appeared like a woman's sexy curves. Yellow rested his calloused hand on its leather seat as the twin cam engine aroused him.

"This isn't like the usual vehicles we catch," he muttered.

Yellow stood up and walked around to admire the bike from a different angle. As he shifted, he saw a desert void. At first, it appeared as if nothing was out of the ordinary, but the fact that the black biker was missing hit Yellow hard. Before his brain's neurons could fire, a sudden blast impaled Yellow's head. His meaty frame toppled to the ground. He tried to collect himself when a cloud covered the sun—a black cloud clad in leather.

"What the hell? I'm gonna get you!" Yellow growled.

Adrenaline pumped through Yellow's widened veins. He jumped up and lunged at the courier, but the leathered individual dodged his attack and countered with a swift kick. Yellow fell. Without thought, he popped up and pounced again. The courier leaned and buckled Yellow's knees sending him back to the unyielding desert.

Yellow lay on the ground as the courier stepped closer to him. The biker's hands raised as Yellow prepared for a final blow, but the individual lifted off the helmet. Time seemed to slow as the long flowing black hair of a fatally attractive woman poured out. She was strong yet feminine, powerful yet graceful, loud yet quiet. Yellow couldn't look, but at the same time, couldn't look away as he studied the woman's curves as he did the pristine motorcycle.

"Who...Who are you?" Yellow mouthed.

"I'm a bitch in heat," the courier's spongy voice expelled. "Where is my bag?"

"Red and Blue took it. What's inside?"

"Rule number one. A courier should never look inside the package."

The courier rested her boot on Yellow's hand. Then, she twisted. Yellow screamed. The courier yanked his yellow bandana as the goon's chubby face breathed the desert air.

"You're as ugly as your rancid stink," she said.

"Wait, I'm just a grunt. Red even said so. Please. What do you want?" Yellow begged.

"I *need* that bag," the courier said, staring at a hole in the sand.

***

Her mind left the barren desert and traveled three hours ago into a smoky bar. The place reeked of body odor as the stale stench of meaty men swirled around the rancid room. A bartender poured a triple shot of whiskey for a slob. Two derelicts shot pool with broken sticks. As the men amused themselves, something cut the light from the doorway. The courier slinked into the bar dressed in sexy leather. The men stopped. Some stared while others catcalled. The courier bumped the slob at the bar as whiskey dumped onto his greasy beard. The bartender backed up as the bar trembled.

"The only bitches allowed in here are whores," the slob roared.

He reached his paws for the courier's neck. She shifted her eyes, and then grabbed his head and smashed his face into the bar. The slob fell over and squirmed.

"You'll never get any with that pick-up line," the courier countered.

Laughter erupted from the other men.

"Tiny got laid out by a chic!" one of the pool players exclaimed.

"Does this bar serve wine?" the courier asked the bartender.

"We have one of the last bottles on the California Island. It's very expensive, ma'am," the bartender explained.

"Get her a glass and put it on my tab," a mysterious voice said.

A white-haired man stood at the bar next to the courier. He wore a perfectly pressed black suit. "I like your style. I have a job for you," the old man said.

"A job? I'm just passing through, old man."

The bartender returned with a bottle of red wine. He uncorked it, and then poured it like a bomb defuser preparing to cut the blue wire. The old man presented the courier with the duffel bag.

"This needs to be delivered to the mainland. Las Vegas. Before dark. To my wife."

The courier glanced at a map hanging on the wall. It showed California, Oregon, and Washington broken away into the ocean from the rest of the United States.

"The mainland, huh? I haven't been there since before the big quake. I hear that drive is full of gangs."

"A lady with your touch shouldn't have a problem navigating," the old man continued.

She took a sip of the wine and massaged her taste buds.

"What are you offering?" she responded, staring at the man with intrigue.

***

A bead of sweat traveled down the courier's face. It was sweat from the sun, which yanked her mind from the vision of the past. She felt the goon squirming under her boot.

"Where are they!?" she demanded as she twisted Yellow's arm with her foot.

He yelped.

"Ugh...two miles that way. Take a right at the painted rock."

She looked in the direction of his gesture as the openness surrounded her.

Meanwhile, some ways up the road, a battered Recreational Vehicle baked under the sun next to a dirt road; the police sedan was parked nearby. The interior of the RV was just as trashed. Refuse littered the beaten brown rugs; bottles of hard liquor cluttered the counters; shovels and pitchforks were scattered on the floor. Near the gutted driver's seat, Red and Blue worked on the duffel bag. Their bandanas hung from their necks exposing their hideous faces. Prickly stubble painted Red's mug as Blue's cleft palate lacked a few teeth.

"Leave it alone! I said I'll do it," Red yelled as he grabbed a rusted saw from Blue.

Red sawed with all his strength, but the bag's armor only taunted him.

"What is that made of?" Blue asked.

"Ah! This damn thing. This has to be some military grade shit."

"This is nothin' like the other stuff we usually get," Blue said, eyeing the collection of wallets, purses, and cell phones stashed in the corner. "Maybe we shouldn't a stopped that guy?"

Red hurled the saw at the empty bottles. Glasses smashed. He dug through the shovels, searching for something, anything, to pierce the bag.

"Watch the booze!" Blue exclaimed as he dodged the flying glass.

"We're bandits. This is what we do. When are you gonna get that through your thick skull?"

"What are you lookin' for?" Blue questioned.

Red ignored his comrade as he grabbed an aerosol can underneath a Twinkie wrapper.

"Let's see how this thing does against some heat," Red said, pulling a lighter from his pocket. "Here, hold the bag."

Blue kept his distance as he extended the duffel bag in his hands. His eyes widened as he watched Red position the aerosol can near his fingers. Red clicked the lighter, and then pressed the can sending flames at the bag. He grunted watching the bag mock the fire. Red flared up just like the flames, as he sprayed savagely in the air.

"Whoa! Watch it! The alcohol!" Blue yelled, ducking.

The sound of the truck entered the RV. Blue peeked through the dry-rotted curtains and saw the parked truck. The courier's bike rested in the bed with the back of Yellow's head showing through the truck's gritty window.

"Boss, Yellow's back."

"Well go out and see if he needs help, you dumb ass."

The duffel bag entertained Red like a lighter to a caveman. Blue followed his order. He pushed open the door as the sun punched him. His eyes adjusted as he made his way toward the truck. The powerful bike intrigued him, but his motionless partner stole his focus. As Blue approached, he noticed Yellow's head resting against the passenger window.

"Yellow? Hey, what you doin' in there?"

Blue grabbed the door's handle, the hot metal scorching his fingers. He didn't flinch as curiosity numbed the pain. He opened the door. Yellow slumped over, his dead eyes locked onto Blue's.

"Oh my God!" Blue erupted.

The terrified hoodlum clamored back until he bumped into something that stole the sun away—the courier. He turned in surprise. The fetching female had a glimmer in her eye. Tied around her neck was the yellow bandana.

"Don't kill me. I'm sorry," Blue cried, running around the RV.

Without hesitating, the courier leaped on top of the truck, and then vaulted off the RV's roof. She eyed the fleeing Blue. Keeping up the momentum, the courier flipped through the air and pierced her boot into Blue's back. He capsized.

"Where's my bag!?" the courier yelled.

"What's inside?" Blue stuttered.

"Rule number one. A courier should never look inside the package. I'm only going to ask you one more time. Where is my bag?"

"Red has it, inside. I told him not to rob you," Blue sobbed.

"I hate it when people lie. If you steal from me, I will steal from you."

The courier snarled her lip as she neared Blue. He kicked up dirt as he tried to retreat. Then, the courier charged forward, grazed his face with her fist, and snatched his blue bandana. She turned as Blue breathed a sigh of relief, but just as quickly, the courier whipped around and dug her boot into his groin, castrating him. Blue lay motionless in pain beyond imagination.

The courier tied the blue bandana around her neck. She stared at the RV in front of her, and then crept around the back. She saw the clouded windows, crisped paint, and flattened tires. She moved slowly and steadily. In front of her was the door. The courier prepared her attack, but then the side window shattered. The courier turned as yellow liquid dumped over her leather outfit. Suddenly, her jacket and pants sizzled.

"How 'bout some battery acid for ya! It didn't work on your bag, but it looks like it's workin' on you!" Red yelled, bursting from the door with his bandana.

As the third bandit darted toward the police car clutching the bag, the courier felt her outer layer melt away. She yanked off her pants and removed her jacket. She tossed the dissolving clothes aside as the sun bathed her skin. A black sports bra and biker shorts accentuated her feminine curves. Her breathtaking body was enough to stop a man in his tracks, but an elusive duffel bag could keep him moving.

Red fired up the sedan and hollered as he spun away. Dust kicked up. The courier clenched her fist, searching for a way to catch him. Then, she saw the truck. It wasn't the hunk of metal that intrigued her; it was the item in the bed—her bike.

The courier bolted toward the crotch rocket. In one swoop, she jumped on top, kick-started it, and then launched off the back. Its twin cams spewed horsepower. The courier rocketed toward the fleeing spot of white. As she winded each gear to the maximum RPM, the wind blew her lustrous hair.

The white police car screamed down the dirt road. Then, it popped onto paved macadam. Sweat beaded on Red's brow. He looked in the rear-view and saw the black dot growing in size.

"Come on, you piece of shit. Move!" Red yelled as he rocked his body, motivating the lazy car.

He saw a connecting road with a sign reading: "Bridge to Las Vegas – 5 miles." The bend seemed too sharp, but Red kept the pedal floored. He hugged the turn. The car's shocks barked. Its tires squealed. Red made the turn as he joined cars on the highway.

"Move it! Get out of my way!" Red shouted as he passed a six-door vehicle.

Red grabbed his last resort—the police light. He stuck it on the roof as his unsteady hand wobbled the car. Red ignited the light and siren at 90 miles an hour.

Wheels spun. The bike banked the turn at full throttle. A look of intent consumed the courier's face as the wind cooled her exposed skin and hardened her nipples. She accelerated on the smooth blacktop, cutting the distance between her and the car.

An elderly couple drove in a solar-powered sedan. As they shuttled along, the enraged police sedan whizzed by.

"Oh my!" the woman said.

"Who's he chasing?" her husband asked.

Suddenly, the courier zipped past, sending waves through their cataracted eyes.

"Yeah, he's got 'em scared. It's 'bout time someone gives the cops a good chase," the elderly man laughed.

Red swerved the car. The courier propelled the bike to the passenger side. Red cut the wheel. The bike pulled back. She powered around to the driver's side. As she reached the door, their eyes locked. The courier glared. Red cowered as he saw the yellow and blue flapping around her neck. Suddenly, Red veered off the road and into the desert.

The car flew on the soft desert sand sending a trail of dust behind it. Red saw the courier slow. He pulled away. A grin painted his ugly mug as he sped through the desert.

Several jeeps were parked in the isolated desert with the words "Seismic Research" plastered on their sides. A reflecting white outfit encased three individuals as they drilled into the desert. Suddenly, the dial on a connected computer oscillated. The workers looked at each other with squinted eyes.

"Is it a quake?" one of them asked.

The researchers turned and saw the police car barreling their way. The three jumped back. Red plowed through. The equipment smashed. They looked back and saw the black crotch rocket approaching. There was nowhere for it to go. They ducked as the bike ramped over a crane and soared above the roused researchers.

Red entered uneven terrain. The car bobbled. Red saw a large solar panel in his direct path. He tried to navigate, but the car surrendered. Red spun the wheel. The car clipped a sand dune and twisted through the air. After nearly two rotations, the car landed on its roof and ground to a stop. Dust engulfed it.

The courier played it safe, watching the wreck from a distance. She saw the dead vehicle, and then accelerated to its side.

Red opened his eyes as sand filled his lungs. Adrenaline flowed through his beaten body as he grabbed the duffel bag and crawled through the side window. He ran toward the solar panel, the red bandana still around his neck.

The courier twisted the throttle. The bike zipped toward Red. She extended her boot and struck his back, sending the bandit plummeting to the sweltering ground.

Red lay on his back. He tried to move but couldn't. His body cried as he tried to focus his eyes, but the sun was too much. The sound of footsteps approached—the loudest footsteps he had ever heard.

"Where are you!?" Red yelled, clutching the duffel bag.

Red rolled over and saw black boots next to him. He followed them up. The sweat on the courier's supple skin glistened. Finally, his sights rested on the woman's inflamed eyes.

"You have something that doesn't belong to you," the courier said.

"Here, you want it. Take it," Red said, tossing the bag ten feet away.

Red scampered in the sand. The courier stood on his hand.

"You know it's not proper for a lady to bend. Now be a good boy and fetch it for me."

Red knew it was futile to resist. He crawled toward the bag, each movement twisting his nerve endings. Red grabbed it.

"Get up and bring it to me," the courier instructed.

Red used all of his strength to stand. He shuffled back to her, one hand holding the duffel bag, the other in his back pocket. Red extended the bag. The courier reached for it, but

Red whipped the tin snips from his pocket, slashing the courier's bra strap. The bag fell. She retreated.

"My momma didn't teach me any manners," Red taunted, waving the snips.

"Now why did you have to go and do that?" the courier said softly as she touched the scrape on her shoulder.

"Are you going to tell me what's inside that thing?" Red demanded.

"Rule number one. A courier should never look inside the package," she replied, shaking her head.

"Come on, sweetie. We can split whatever's in there."

"You saw what happened to your friends. So I suggest you back off."

"Let's head back to the Kremlin. I have some Southern-style moonshine," Red continued.

"You really know how to woo a lady."

"Now listen! There's nothin' in this world I'd rather see other than what's in that bag," Red snarled.

And then, the courier raised her hand and gripped her most potent weapon—her bra. She pulled the other strap and exposed her sun-kissed C-cup. Red's mouth dropped as well as the tin snips.

"You wanna touch them? This body's all real," the courier hummed as she snaked toward him.

Her breasts filled Red's eyes. His hand trembled as he inched toward the pink nipple teasing him. He cut the inches, moving closer and closer. Without hesitation, the courier kicked the snips in the air, grabbed them, and then sliced off three fingers from the protruding hand. Red fell, howling, as she snatched his red bandana.

The courier nonchalantly trekked to the bag, grabbed it, and then returned to her bike. She turned to the weeping bandit.

"I told you that it's not polite to make a woman bend."

The courier secured the bag on the back, but realized the lock was open. She stopped breathing for a moment. The open flap burned into her eyes. Finally, she reached inside the bowels of the bag. She grabbed its contents and removed them. It was packs of paper held tightly by a clip. The faces of ex-Presidents didn't cover them, but rather items of food. They were packs of coupons. The courier fanned through them seeing fifty cents off laundry detergent, seventy-five cents discount on dishwasher soap, and free mini-size peanut butter crackers. Her eyes squinted as a ticket fell from the bag. The courier mouthed it aloud.

"Sandy Midler – Great Granddaughter of Bette Midler – Seating by Dark."

A crow squawked in the sky. The courier put the items back into the bag, secured it on the bike, and then hopped on. She kick-started the crotch rocket and blasted away, without looking back.

Wheels spun on blacktop. Black boots rested on pegs inches from the speeding pavement. Black bikini bottoms enveloped the courier as her soft skin radiated. The red, yellow, and blue bandanas covered her plump breasts. A grin painted her face as she commanded the bike.

The bike zipped across a huge suspension bridge. Water surrounded a metropolis. Skyscrapers reached for the cloudless blue sky. The courier weaved between solar-powered cars. She saw a sign that read "Las Vegas Strip – Straight, Las Vegas Shipyards – Next Right." The courier pulled a wheelie and continued straight toward the action under the setting sun.

I'm back. Sorry it took so long. My snack didn't want to cooperate. I see the cash register looks the same. I knew I'd be the only sucker tonight.

What did you think about that story? Now that's a crazy bitch. Las Vegas is headed for the big one. We're living in a place where Mother Nature didn't intend millions of people to live.

Well, I've got good news. It's closing time! Let's get this cart shut down and the money counted. I'll read you the next story as we work. I know it all too well.

Beyond the Strip

Have you ever felt trapped? I needed to get out of this coffin. I was driving for too long. The smell of these cardboard boxes was toxic. As the desert seemed endless, the light suddenly hit me; it illuminated the night sky. There it was, the sign I had been dying to see.

"Welcome to Fabulous Las Vegas," I muttered, reading it aloud.

I pulled into a spot and checked my vanity mirror. How did I make it? I saw my brunette hair draped over my bloodshot eyes. But everything was behind me now.

Tourists stood in line to get a picture. A husband and wife embraced as a camera captured them at the start of the Las Vegas Strip. Finally, it was my turn. I held the magazine in my hands that had brought me here. I gave my camera to an eager man. He told me to smile, but I was already.

A ring blasted from somewhere. It pierced my ears. Where was it coming from? A camera nearby flashed. The light consumed me. I couldn't see, but then something came into my view. It was the intense color of red—blood red. As my mind raced, I quickly realized the color was from the display on my alarm clock. I was in my bedroom, awakened from a dream.

The ring blasted again from my cell phone, which roused not only me, but also my baby. He began to cry as I reached for him. He was my life now, and he was all that I had left after losing my way. I picked him up and cradled him in my arms.

"Oh, my sweet baby," I whispered.

The phone barked again as my little boy howled. I jumped to answer the pest.

"Yeah," I said.

"Where's my money?" the deep voice said—the last voice I wanted to hear.

"Soon," I replied.

"Listen, bitch. Give me my fuckin' money—"

I threw the phone against the wall. I held my boy tightly.

"Shhhh," I exhaled into his ear.

As I rocked him, I glanced around my studio apartment. Clothes were sprawled everywhere. A roach, also awakened by the noise, crawled on the wall. The kitchen was bare. I closed my eyes, escaping from this hellhole. What happened to me? Why was I dealt these cards? I missed my mom now more than ever, but that life in the city was over. I needed to find a completely new path; I needed to find a way out.

My baby's cries subsided to grunts. He was drifting asleep. I combed his soft hair, painted his slippery skin with my fingertip, and then kissed him softly. I hoped he was dreaming of a happy place, removed from this nightmare of reality.

I positioned him down in his crib like placing the last rose of the season into a vase. Suddenly, the phone rang again. I clutched the pest and yanked its battery out. As I readjusted the black sheets over my window, a twinge tickled my brain. It was happening again. Spots of light filled my eyes as my head screamed. I massaged my temples, but I knew only one thing could pacify the pain. Rummaging through a pile of clothes, I dug past a bra and found a pill bottle between panties crusted with dried cum. I popped four pills this time.

I showered, letting the warm water cleanse me. I shaved my legs with my unsteady hand, shaking from my drug-induced sense of calm. The razor traveled over my knee, but then I felt it slice my calf. Blood oozed from the open wound. All I could do was watch the red swirl down the drain.

I dressed the way men wanted me to dress, the way that put a spark in their crotch and a sizzle in my pocketbook. I transformed into a character, one who was carefree and seductive. I pushed aside oozing toiletries as I tried to find a Band-Aid for my cut. Through the mess, I found one that was unused. After covering the wound, I drew a black pencil on my eyes like some morbid artist nearing suicide. My bleached blonde hair looked ratty, the brown roots of my past invading. But my hair was usually the last thing that men really cared about. I pushed up my breasts and glared at the hideous woman in front of me.

I held my baby in my arms as if it were the last time. Who knew? With him cradled, I tiptoed out of the apartment and knocked on my neighbor's door.

"Be home. Be home," I sighed.

Suddenly, the door crept open as the elderly woman peeked out in her bathrobe. I didn't even know her name, but it didn't matter. I knew she understood my situation, and after seeing that withered tattoo on her wrist, perhaps she understood it all too well.

"Sorry. Can I ask a favor?" I said.

"Not another night."

"I have to work. Need to pay rent."

The elderly woman shook her head, but then looked at my baby boy in my arms. She smiled as only a mother would smile. Then, she scooped him up.

"You're so beautiful," the elderly woman said to my baby.

We both stared at my boy, sleeping without a care in the world.

I found my way to the lights. The Las Vegas Strip was a bizarre place. Creatures from all holes in the Earth seemed to find their way to this oxymoron in the desert. The city touted itself as a place to hide, a place where all your transgressions would stay. But for those who had escaped their past to find a better life, their transgressions would only pile higher as the city ate away at them like a cancer. I too fell into its trap.

I slinked on the sidewalk in front of the casinos. Families roamed; drunks exited a cab; headlights flowed. The lights had attracted hundreds of creatures. Any and every one could be a customer. I always looked at a man's watch as a gauge for his wallet.

A white-haired man meandered my way.

"Need a date?" I asked glancing at his sterling silver wristwatch, but he didn't take the bait.

I passed the piles of adult material littering the street easily mistaken for baseball cards to a kid. Who said Las Vegas didn't have its own sports team? Up ahead, three college guys stumbled my way. One had a shaved head that reflected the lights of the casinos. A burly guy with a full beard laughed next to him as a tall one with dorky glasses followed. I watched the two jocks in front sip their beers. College guys were the easiest target. They usually had the most energy, and cummed the fastest. I could get through three or four of them on a good night. On the other hand, older men required more work. It was like going to a cheap diner where you had to not only eat the stale eggs, but cook them too.

I stood tall, brought my shoulders back, and swayed my hips toward them.

"Hey, boys," I purred.

They stopped with their tails up.

"Here we go," the bearded man said.

"Not bad," the hairless guy added.

"What are you boys up to tonight?" I asked, slithering a few feet off the beaten path.

"How much?" the one with the facial hair asked.

"It's not nice to ask a lady her age."

"Come on. How much for an hour? All three of us," the jock with the shaved head asked.

A beer bottle half empty was a call girl's best friend, but one nearly empty was her worst enemy. And these guys only had one gulp left.

"You guys are drunk," I said.

"Come on, baby. I thought whores love forward guys."

"Fuck you!" I barked, pushing my way past them.

As I stomped away, I saw the bearded guy pull something out of his pants. I was ready to add these guys to the list that included the vomiting virgin at the sight of my C-cup, but then I saw him holding the color green in his hand.

"Come on. One hour..."

I stared at the cash in his hands.

The walk to the room was always the most uncomfortable. It felt like it did when I was a teenager, going to confession with my dad while wearing my hip huggers. But once the curtain closed, the deed got done. These guys were staying at the cheapest hotel on the Strip. We shifted up to their room as the two leaders joked as if I weren't even there. The one who worried me the most was the quiet one, still holding back. When the door shut, the quiet ones were usually the loudest.

As soon as the door closed, the two pilots threw me on the bed as my purse fell to the ground. I stared at the money on the nightstand as they ravished me. Their meaty hands felt like spiders crawling over my exposed skin. One ripped my top off. Another yanked my skirt down tearing the Band-Aid from my skin. The wound throbbed, but the money on the nightstand helped to ease the pain. Then, the quiet one spoke.

"Guys. Come on. This isn't why I came to Vegas."

His voice was like a restful breeze through a restless room. I glanced at him. He had picked up my purse as well as a picture that had flown from inside. Without even seeing the front, I knew it was the only picture I had kept inside my handbag—a picture of my son.

"Leave her alone!" the nerdy guy barked.

The bearded jock, the monster, lunged at the voice of reason.

"Go find your own whore if you don't like this one!" he screamed.

"Get him out of here!" blasted from the guy still on top of me.

The jock pitched his buddy out of the room. Then, I was all alone to finish my business transaction.

Hours had passed, too many to count. The sun was ready to rise as I found my way beyond the Strip to the place that I called home. Even though my bra was filled with money, all I cared about was seeing the only thing I had left.

I knocked on my neighbor's apartment. Seconds passed, which seemed like hours. A man dressed for work stepped by me. I didn't look at him, yet I knew he was looking at me.

"Open the door. Open the fucking door," I said under my breath.

Finally, the door listened. The elderly woman locked eyes with me, as I knew the dried black tears on my face startled her. But there he was still pacified. I held my son tightly.

The days replicated—more makeup, more nights away from my boy, more horny tourists with deep pockets. I tried to save money, tried not to buy more things to deaden the pain, but my money dwindled. Something was going to break, and then one night my shrinking black eyeliner did.

I returned to the elderly woman at some awful hour after a night of sin. She opened the door but didn't hold out my baby. She clutched him as only I did.

"This has to stop. I'm gonna have to call child services."

"No! It's okay. I'm starting a new job tomorrow. I'm fine," I lied.

"I don't believe you."

"I'm sorry. I won't bother you again. Can I just have my baby back?" I pleaded.

Cries poured from my boy. I grabbed him from her arms and fumbled my way into my apartment. I slammed the door.

"Shhh, my baby. Shhh," I said, rocking him in my arms.

My apartment was a toilet. I needed to get out of here, but where would I go? As I stood just past the door, the smell of burned tobacco punched my face. My baby kicked and screamed. My brain throbbed. I set him on the couch, and then trekked into the kitchen, searching for my fix. I sifted through a pile of energy bar wrappers. I opened the fridge; a can of tuna and baby formula stared at me. Then, I saw a pill bottle on the floor. I reached for it, but a cockroach scurried out. I stared at the bug. I knew it had stolen my pills. I tried to catch the fleeing insect.

"Get back here," I commanded the roach.

It scurried under the refrigerator. I had to get it.

"Please, give me a pill," I begged the cockroach.

Suddenly, a shadow shifted. I looked at my baby, but he was gone. I followed his cries and saw him clutched by arms painted with tattoos. It was the last place I wanted him to be.

"What is more important? This or this?" the same voice from the phone asked holding my baby in one hand and a bottle of pills in the other.

The question did not register.

"What are you fuckin' doing? Give my baby back!" I demanded, thrusting toward him.

He lifted my boy above his head. I froze.

"You haven't paid me for these," he replied, a cigarette dangling from his mouth.

"I'll get you the money!"

"You said that last time."

He inhaled the cigarette; the red dot intensified. I held my breath as if I were watching some kind of twisted horror film. He lowered my baby, and then blew smoke into his face.

"It'd be a shame if something happened to him."

"You asshole!" I barked, lunging at the thug, but he tossed me to the ground.

"Go get me my money, bitch!" he roared.

I couldn't hold back the tears. My life flashed before me. It felt like only yesterday I was sitting on my dad's lap as mom baked in the kitchen. But now, I was on the floor, sitting on a vomit stain. I looked into the kitchen, but my mom wasn't there.

"Please give me my baby," I whispered through the tears.

"You have two hours. Go out and get my fuckin' money," the beast continued.

"Let me get the neighbor to watch him," I offered, reaching for my precious child.

"I'll watch him. I always liked kids," he replied, blowing more smoke into my baby's face.

I cried even more than my baby boy.

"Just so you don't get any ideas about bringing the cops back. You know what they'd do to a crack mother," he said, throwing a bag of rocks on my couch.

I had nowhere to go, no plan, no light to guide me. I had to negotiate with this piece of trash, but then again, I too was not much better. I was a failed mother forced to leave her baby in the arms of evil.

There were thousands of people on the Strip, yet it was lifeless. I stumbled down the sidewalk, makeup smeared on my face. I knew I was unattractive, yet I had to be attractive. I looked at every man, hoping one would take my bait. A married couple wandered. Asian tourists snickered. Drunks yelled. I kept moving until I saw someone see me. It was a dark, menacing man, but I didn't care.

An hour went by that I couldn't even describe. That customer was rough, too rough. My eye had nearly swollen shut from the punch he had given me, but it didn't matter. I made it out alive with money. I ran home still yearning for my little boy. How could I leave him with that monster?

I opened the door. Smoke billowed. Finally, I saw my baby. He was happy, smiling with a toy. But as I approached, I realized the toy in his mouth was a pistol.

"You look like shit... Now. Where's my fuckin' money?" the voice snarled from the shadows.

"Take that gun from my baby's mouth," I insisted.

"Money! Bitch!" he yelled standing between me and my boy.

I handed him the bills from my bra.

"This is it? *This* is fuckin' it?" he yapped, throwing me down.

"I need more time."

He pulled the pistol from my baby's mouth. I crawled toward his helpless body. Then, my attacker dug the hard barrel into my skull.

"I'm tired of your shit! What should stop me from pulling the trigger? Huh? Huh!?"

My baby screamed.

"You leave me no choice. I have to take him," he said as he scooped up my son.

"No! You can have me. Fuck me if you want!" I blasted.

"Your pussy won't pay for my spinners."

I lunged at him with all my energy. I touched my baby's delicate arm. But then, the arm covered with tattoos flung me aside. My leg bent. A boot flew off. Then, I felt something bash my head. The room went dim, sound muffled, but I still heard my baby crying, which motivated me to hang on. I stood up and saw the hoodlum dashing from my apartment. My heart pounded. I ran, but my bootless bare foot mocked me. I removed the other boot and exploded from the room. The hoodlum walked down the steps holding my life in his hands. I couldn't let him go. I wielded the heel on my boot as a weapon and dove down the stairway. I stabbed the 200-pound man in his eye. Finally, he relinquished his grip as I clutched my baby. The beast roared. I saw the elderly woman open her apartment and for a split second, she saw me at my worst.

"Get back here, bitch!"

I snuck past him and darted toward the door. The cool desert air hit me. My baby squirmed as I looked left, and then right, but the night had stolen the life from the street. Suddenly, I saw a couple turn the corner.

"Help me!" I yelled, but they taunted me with ignorance.

I heard the creature stomping my way. Police sirens approached from somewhere. A man watched from across the street, and then turned around. I was all alone. I ran barefoot toward the only thing I knew—the lights.

I made it two blocks and entered the Strip. I was now back at the bowels of America, the playground for the illicit. I looked behind me and saw the animal continuing his hunt. I thought about the police, but there were too many questions down that path. I needed to escape from this mess, to take cover in the crowd to find my way out of the city. But at this hour, I knew those who could help were off in some distant land, dreaming in their beds.

I ran into a casino entryway, but saw the security force just past the doorway. I turned back and ran, but then suddenly, I saw someone approaching. I couldn't catch my breath. I couldn't think. I couldn't react. I could only watch as I beheld the face of the being. Then, my heart stopped as I saw the glasses of that dorky guy. He had a look of compassion in his eyes, a look that would forever be in my memory.

"What's wrong?" he asked.

I didn't respond. All I did was fall into his open arms.

People smiled around me. Kids laughed. Families embraced. My hair blew in my eyes. It was the color brown. The cameraman waved at me. I smiled as I held up the item that had motivated me to leave my life back East. He took my picture. Then, I turned and saw the sign welcoming me to fabulous Las Vegas. It was breathtaking. I glanced at the item in my hand—the magazine ad. I read it under my breath.

"Come To Las Vegas – Be A Showgirl – The Place Where Opportunity Is Everywhere."

Suddenly, a ring sounded. It overwhelmed the laughter around me. It blasted again in my ears as a camera flash showered me with light.

I jarred awake inside a car. It was that dream again. My arms were empty as I looked for my baby boy. There he was sleeping in a car seat next to a pile of hospital scrubs.

"Sorry," a voice said silencing the ringing cell phone.

I turned and saw my savior, the guy with the glasses, driving away from the lights.

"No... *I'm* sorry," I muttered as I kissed his hand tenderly.

We were leaving this bizarre city. Las Vegas was like a flower offering its sweet nectar to the world. But some flowers used this nectar as a way to attract its unsuspecting victims.

I saw the back of the sign that had lured me here one year ago.

"Drive Carefully – Come Back Soon."

A little girl darted from the sign and into the road. We stopped suddenly. I watched as her parents ran out and scooped her up. It made me think of my parents. Why did they have to leave me so soon? I glanced at the grass mound in front of the Welcome sign. A young girl my age stood all alone. She was smiling.

Sad stories are food for the soul. These lights around us are bright, but they can burn out quickly.

Well, we're done. It's eleven o'clock in Las Vegas. It's the start of another night of sin. I have to run this money to the office. You still want to come, right? Come on. You're not finished with the book. There are still a lot more good stories. You came here by bus, huh? Well then, you must come with me. I'll drive us. Stick with me tonight. You can help me with my gig. I'll introduce you to my group. It'll be fun.

I parked at the Planet Hollywood. We have a twenty-minute walk in this heat. It's eleven o'clock and it's still ninety degrees. Isn't it great! The next story is something much lighter. We need something lighter after that last one.

The Water Princess

The sun burned out a rain cloud. An SUV drove out of the city. Inside sat a young girl named Emily Swenson. Emily was a special nine-year-old girl. She wasn't special because of her cute and innocent personality or her love for the water, but for the magical world that she and her family were about to move to. Her family left the eclectic New York City destined for upstate. Emily was used to frequent trips on the subway, walks with her mother in Central Park, and tri-weekly swim team meets that she grew to love. Although on the outside she was reserved, Emily craved the engrossing city just a few steps away from her downtown apartment, even if she preferred just to be a bystander.

Kate, Emily's mother, was quaint. She worked part-time at the local library branch, but her main job was to be a mom. She loved Emily beyond herself and knew that although her daughter may be introverted, she was special. Kate didn't miss any of Emily's swim meets and ensured that her daughter was always early, dressed in her swimsuit. Emily craved the water. She felt like a different person submerged in H2O. She was no longer shy, but active and outgoing like a free fish.

Her father, Vincent, was a well-respected college instructor who was the kind of guy whom everybody liked. Unfortunately, he was an adjunct instructor of history making ends meet for his family by picking up a class to teach here or there. He tried to get on full-time at the community colleges, but had no luck. Then one day, he had two offers for Associate Professor—one at a college in Las Vegas and the other at a university in upstate New York. Vincent had reservations about raising a family in Sin City. Therefore, his choice was simple. He packed up the family's cramped apartment and decided to move to the small community of Greenview in the mountains of New York.

Emily felt nervous about leaving what she knew. She was no longer in an environment that she understood—no longer with her favorite coach or the other girls on her team.

The drive seemed long to Emily. She peered out the SUV's window as the scenery turned from cement buildings to wooded trees. As her parents conversed about the mountainous vista, Emily listened with headphones to her favorite New York City radio station. But as the miles added up, the station crackled and faded, and eventually withered away to static air. She wanted to hold on to as much of her past as she could before the new town disrupted her status quo.

The large and mystic sign came into view, "Greenview Estates." Vincent grew excited at the start of the cobblestone road that he knew would lead home from work every day.

Kate took in the new environment feeling a bittersweet emotion—sweet from Vincent's obvious exuberance, but bitter from Emily's hidden apprehension.

As the SUV crept down the cobblestone road, the towering homes dwarfed the family's view. The aged structures sat thirty yards back inside huge lots fit for America's version of British aristocrats.

"There's no way we could've afforded one of these in the city on a professor's salary," Vincent said.

Kate turned to the back seat where little Emily sat surrounded by boxes. She flailed her arms trying to pry Emily's attention from her headphones.

"We're here, honey," Kate shouted.

Emily admired the tall oak trees and green brush. It was as if the monstrous house in front of her was not even there.

"There's nothing here," she quietly remarked.

Emily looked down at her lap and took a deep breath. She studied the swim team photo that her bubbly teammates gave her as a token of their time together.

Vincent drove up the long gravel driveway to their new abode. The mammoth white house had two long pillars guarding the front door. The house looked like a painting that had aged from contemporary art to an ageless masterpiece. Vincent eagerly hopped out while Kate focused on opening the door for Emily. As the nine-year-old stepped onto the rocky ground, she knew that she was far away from the city.

She gazed into the backyard, captivated by the wooded area overshadowing the gigantic house.

"I miss home," Emily sadly remarked as she sulked to the front door.

She sat on the stoop. Kate and Vincent stared at her from a distance, saddened by how the house seemed to overwhelm her.

"I hope she makes some friends here," Kate mumbled.

Emily's room was huge, quite different from the confined space in their apartment. She sat on the freshly delivered mattress, unpacking some of her favorite fairy tales. Emily thought about all the nights that her mother had read her to sleep. As her mind drifted from her new room, Vincent surprised her with another large box. Then just as quickly, he scurried back down to unload even more. Emily studied the clunky box, knowing it contained her most prized possessions. She carefully opened it revealing three of her swimming trophies, one of which was for taking city champion in the youth fifty-meter breaststroke. The thought of her swim team and the months of practice for that competition saddened her. Emily had to walk away from the glimmering gold to keep from crying.

Emily decided to explore the overpowering room. Musty air filled her nose and the dust clouded her eyes as she examined the side of the brick chimney. Finally, she arrived at the old closet door. It creaked as she opened it. Emily reached through the darkness to yank the dangling string. The light bulb illuminated the stale space and sent a bolt of intensity to her eyes. Emily looked down, but then suddenly shrieked. A dead cockroach stared back at her, shriveled from months of death. Emily hated bugs, even though the city was notorious for them. She stomped on the roach, ensuring to destroy any remote chance of a revival. As the crunch of the shriveled insect echoed in the confined space, an anomalous board caught the curious girl's eye. Emily kneeled and pried up the board with her little fingers. There was a hiding spot! She reached in and felt something hard. It moved free as Emily used all of her strength to pull out the concealed item—a dusty old book.

Taking her new prize into the ray of sun resting on her bed, she realized that the item she held came from a very different time and place. The title, *The Tale of Tall Oaks,* captivated her with its fancy font. As she blew the dust off the book's cover, Emily opened it revealing a colorful array of mystical creatures popping up a few inches from the page.

"Did I hear you scream?" Kate inquired as she entered Emily's room.

Emily explained about the icky dead bug, but the mystic book quickly changed Kate's focus. The little pop-ups were a carefully crafted masterpiece with intricate design and color, albeit faded from age.

"Is it a fairy tale?" Kate asked as she studied the bizarre book even closer.

"I think," Emily replied.

Kate promised to read to her before bed, but her motherly duties trumped Emily's find. She whisked her daughter to the bathroom to tidy up from her dusty adventure before dinner. As Emily walked out of the room, Kate took a moment to reflect on the interesting treasure that the sprawling room had concealed.

Later that night after the moon had encroached on the arcane house, Kate put the final changes on transforming

Emily's room into something familiar. The vibrant polka-dot sheets and eye-grabbing curtains brightened the otherwise bleak room. Emily ran in from brushing her teeth, excited to have her mother read her to sleep. The nine-year-old didn't hesitate as she jumped into bed. Her mother tucked her in snuggly just as she did every night. As Emily lay on her familiar sheets, Kate slowly picked up the book, intriguing her daughter. Kate opened the first page and read aloud the title, adding a little mystery to her normally dainty voice, "The Tale of Tall Oaks."

"This is the story of a magical world covered by lavish green mountains. It was called Land of Tall Oaks. And the ruler and protector of this magical land was the beautiful Princess Tattlebee."

Kate flipped the page revealing a princess wearing a dress made from a rainbow of colors. The princess had tanned skin and long brown hair crowned by a sparkling headdress.

She continued, "All the slimy and slithery creatures of this land worshiped Princess Tattlebee and showered her with beautiful treasures hidden deep within the magical woods."

Kate turned the withered page. A brown creature shaped like a walnut with wings greeted them. And right in the middle of his body was a single big eye. The creature seemed alive as it protruded from the page.

"An army of little Stubbies offered guidance and protection to Princess Tattlebee. While Stubbies appeared scary at first with their one eye, they were the most fun creatures in the land. They played with the others and were able to fly to the tops of trees to harvest food for everyone.

But most importantly, these creatures ensured Princess Tattlebee maintained control over the blissful mountains."

As Kate flipped the page again, an evil shark-like creature snarled off the page. Its eyes glared and its fins appeared like blades.

"However, pockets of deep water sat throughout this world and were inhabited by evil Subdwellers with deadly jaws. Princess Tattlebee could never enter these bodies of water, as her powers of good were useless against these hungry sea creatures. Thus, Princess Tattlebee must always travel with Stubbies to help guide her way."

Kate paused looking at her sleeping daughter cradled in her lap. She carefully laid the book down on the nightstand, keeping it open to where she had left off. The little Stubbies still protruded from the page staring at the sleeping Emily. Kate tiptoed out of the room leaving her daughter alone in a dream.

Later that night when the moon shined at its brightest, an eerie creak filled Emily's room. The warm summer breeze picked up. The window curtains flowed. Suddenly, an old, crackled voice spoke, "Emily, wake up, wake up."

Emily wearily opened her eyes from the strange voice. She immediately noticed the old book sitting on her nightstand. Surprisingly, the Stubby was mysteriously missing.

"Over here," the voice echoed.

Emily looked down at the floor where the lively Stubby peered at her. Emily wasn't afraid. In fact, she was intrigued at the sight.

"Where did you come from?" she said.

"I came from the Land of Tall Oaks on a mission from Princess Tattlebee."

Emily widened her eyes.

"Outside in the magical woods, come quickly!" he instructed.

Before Emily could pose another question, the little Stubby floated out of her window and into the backyard. Emily sprang from bed and carefully left her room, sneaking through the night toward the back door.

The crickets playfully chirped under the full moon. Emily opened the door to the backyard. She stepped down, feeling the soft blades of grass tickle her little toes. Searching for the Stubby, she made her way toward the back of the yard at the start of the massive woods. Out of nowhere, the Stubby floated from behind an oak tree.

"Back here. Further..."

"What do I have to do?" she questioned.

"Princess Tattlebee knows you're a very special girl and she has entrusted you with a very important task. We have to find the hidden key."

The task riddled Emily with curiosity as she searched the area behind the Stubby.

"What does it look like?" she asked.

The little creature quickly floated around the area as little Emily struggled to keep up.

"Here it is!" the critter exclaimed.

Emily ran behind a tall oak tree. She examined the ground for the hidden treasure, but all she saw was a uniquely shaped rock the size of a walnut.

"Pick it up and keep it with you at all times," the little Stubby explained.

The odd rock appeared innocuous like any other piece of earth, but it did have a distinctive point on one end.

"I must go now, Princess Tattlebee is counting on you," the Stubby said as he floated away toward Emily's window.

Emily stood in the dirt holding the new treasure. She thought about the secret mission that was entrusted to her, but the lack of direction only confused her. Her questions quickly subsided as the floodlights from the house illuminated the backyard.

"Emily!?" her parents yelled searching for their missing daughter.

Emily hid the rock in her pajama pocket and dashed toward the light.

"I'm over here!"

Vincent and Kate ran toward her and checked her face and hands, noticing the dirt on her skin.

"What are you doing out here?" Vincent asked.

"Uh. I just couldn't sleep. I wanted to explore."

"It's the middle of the night. Don't do this again. You scared us," Kate said.

Vincent and Kate held Emily tightly, concerned over their daughter's strange behavior.

The next morning Emily began reading the old book the minute she opened her eyes. She brought it with her as she dressed, and then kept it on the table next to her breakfast. Vincent and Kate noticed Emily engrossed in the book as she sat at the temporary kitchen table eating her cereal.

"I'm worried about her. I think she needs some other kids to play with," Kate whispered to Vincent.

As Vincent unpacked a large box, he too felt guilty for ripping Emily away from the place she had called home for the nine years of her life.

"What can Emily do to make new friends?" he muttered.

An idea popped into his head. He leaned over to Kate. "Why don't you take her to the mall?"

Kate smiled and thought that was a splendid idea.

The bustling mall hopped with families enjoying a day of shopping. A large indoor play area occupied the center crosswalk next to the food court. Emily sat with Kate at a small table next to an ice cream kiosk, which gave way to a bunch of kids Emily's age. As Kate looked at the kids playing, she returned her eyes to Emily still reading the old book.

"Do you want some ice cream?" Kate asked.

Emily shook her head, unconcerned with ice cream or even the kids surrounding her with laughs. It would take a great deal to overcome her fear of meeting new people and entering new places. But the book offered her an escape, a place that she felt at home and in control, and more importantly, entrusted with a secret shared by no one.

Later that night, Vincent and Kate continued their daunting mission of unpacking and organizing their new house. As they worked, they kept an eye on Emily sitting in the living room, still studying her newfound book. Kate told Vincent about their day at the mall and the inability for any of the other kids to penetrate her much guarded shell. Vincent and Kate discussed other events and locations to help ease Emily into the new town.

An idea clicked inside Kate's head.

"Emily. Can you please come here?" Kate called.

"What, mommy?" Emily asked. She sprang from the chair and scurried into the kitchen.

Kate smiled at her daughter and offered a suggestion. "Do you want to go swimming tomorrow?"

Emily immediately brightened up from her mother's question, but just as fast, she reversed her feelings at the realization that the public pool would bring an army of unfamiliar faces. Emily agreed to go with a hesitated nod, but knew she would stay close to her parents, and more importantly, her special book.

The large outdoor pool baked under the hot summer sun as kids and parents splashed in the refreshing water. Emily sat in between her mother and father. She felt uneasy about the new location. Vincent and Kate tried to do their best to ease Emily into the new environment. They offered to go in the water with her, even though neither cared to.

Kate looked down at her little daughter sitting in her bright yellow one-piece. She smiled in such a way that only mothers knew. She studied her daughter's sun-kissed freckles, red nail polish, and perfectly pulled-back ponytail when something caught her eye. It was the strange rock.

"What is that strange necklace you've been wearing?" Kate asked.

Emily grasped the rock dangling from her neck on a shoelace. She thought about that night, and the excitement she had in finding the secret treasure, even if the opportunity to use it had never surfaced. Before Emily could muster a response, a loud whistle erupted from the deep end of the pool.

"A boy is caught under the water!" a woman screamed in the crowd.

Everyone rubbernecked, blindsided by the two lifeguards diving into the water. While everyone froze, Emily knew this was her calling. The winner of the NYC fifty-meter breaststroke clutched the rock and instinctively dove into the water, rhythmically swimming toward the danger. Emily navigated around the many bodies all frozen in the water from uncertainty. As she neared the boy, she could see his leg caught inside the grate at the bottom of the deep end. The grate grew as she approached. Suddenly, its four distinct bars resembled the jaws of the evil Subdwellers from *The Tale of Tall Oaks*. It was as if they sucked and fed on the boy's leg. The two lifeguards did their best to try to free the boy, but their drive seemed useless. The boy flailed his arms. The lifeguards screamed. Emily swam faster. After a battle for air, the boy's body went limp. Emily reached the danger and grabbed the special rock. She slid the unique pointed end into the anomalous bolt holding the grate closed. It fit perfectly. Emily gave it a few quick turns. Suddenly, the jaws of the grate popped open freeing the boy.

The lifeguards pulled the boy up. As they arose from the water, the awaiting crowd gasped from the boy's lifeless body. Quickly, they rolled him onto the concrete and performed mouth-to-mouth resuscitation. They did their best to revive him. Each second seemed like an hour as the crowd remained mute. Then all of a sudden, the boy coughed and filled his lungs with much needed air. The young boy's parents cut through the crowd and held their revived son in their arms.

"Where is the girl who saved him?" the lifeguards yelled at the crowd.

Everyone turned in admiration at the bashful Emily sitting calmly on the edge of the pool. It was as if she knew all along that the boy would be saved. Several young girls and boys, Emily's age, ran up to her and patted her on the back.

"I never met a hero...my name is Billy...I'm Stacy," the kids said.

Vincent and Kate proudly watched their daughter glowing, as she was now the center of attention. Back in the deserted shallow end, Emily's book lay open with the little Stubby protruding from the page. All of a sudden the creature moved and gave a hint of a smile, knowing its job to guide Emily was now finished.

From that day forward, Emily was the talk of the small town where all the kids wanted to meet, as the local paper called her, "The Water Princess." And every night before bed, Emily kept her newfound book near her side, protecting the secrets of the magical Tall Oaks.

Planet Hollywood parking garage
11:29 p.m.

Aw... To be young again. I wonder what would have happened to little Emily if her dad took the job in Vegas.

Just move that stuff from the front seat. I know it's a compact car, but it's all I can afford at the moment. The office is behind the Strip. That's probably where you were interviewed. You *were* the new salesperson, right? Hell, I don't really care. I like you. You're already a friend.

It's a short distance, but a long drive with all these tourists. There's a flavor of everyone wandering these streets. There's the retired couple after an evening of right arm exercise. Walking over there is the family lured by the false advertising. And getting out of that limo are some conference guys ready to explore the city's shadows.

Speaking of conference guys, you've got to read the next story. We have time. I need to fill up this car for our trip.

Political Jungle

The steaming hot coffee consumed the powerless sugar. Harry Stevenson sipped the concoction as he sat toward the back of the packed conference room, trying to stay awake. A gray-haired man babbled about government ethics and while Harry's body was physically in the room, his mind was thinking of his wife three time zones away. Harry was a good-looking man, the type who women liked to watch work out at the gym. He was aged gracefully thirty-eight years, and was the father of two teenage daughters with his high-school sweetheart. He was a newly minted politician, a freshman congressman from his state in the Northeast. Three months prior, he had won the election to his state legislature and had a lot to learn about the ins and outs of politics. Harry was no stranger to the government; in fact, his uncle served for a decade in the state Senate, but the day-to-day aspects of his leadership position were still a learning experience. A graduate of a Big Ten school with a Juris Doctorate, moving from a criminal defense lawyer to a house representative would seem like a natural transition. However, the endless votes, loud cocktail parties, and mundane conferences were beginning to irk him and his family, even though he had just taken office. Nevertheless, Harry knew the power and respect the position would bring as time passed.

"That wraps up my presentation. Any questions from the audience?" asked the gray-haired man on stage.

The audience remained mute. Harry figured they were probably thinking the same thing, "Eight hours at a government leadership conference were enough for one day." The fact that the conference was in fabulous Las Vegas was probably the reason everyone signed up, which, of course, lured Harry. He had never been to Las Vegas, and neither had his family for that matter, but a few days away to explore, he concluded, wouldn't hurt anyone.

Harry filed out of the convention center and waited in the bloated taxi line. He thought about spending some time investigating his hotel, something he did not get a chance to do with his late flight the previous night. Then like a mistuned cello, a deep rasp filled his ears. "Harry, how's it going? Do you want to share a cab back?"

It was Oliver Gaspy, a state senator from the South. The man was a middle-aged burly fellow, a politician for twenty years, and would probably be for twenty more. He was a loud man, the type that was probably shushed in church when he whispered his prayers. Harry wasn't too fond of his political colleague. The senator from the South rubbed him the wrong way at lunch when he boasted about the call girl that he had accosted the night before.

"Uh. Actually, I think I may walk. I've been sitting in that room for too long today," Harry responded in an attempt to rid himself of the seedy man.

"Excellent! I'll join you. We're both staying at the Stratosphere."

Those were the last words that Harry wanted to hear, but he had already dug his hole and there was no easy way to get out of it.

"Okay, sounds good," Harry lied.

Both men walked the one-mile journey from the convention center to the Stratosphere. They resembled two fish out of water as they trekked down the sidewalk, dressed in business suits with conference badges around their necks. Their route was one rarely traveled by tourists, and as they passed several shady characters, Harry almost wished he had said "yes" to the dodgy man's initial request.

"So you've been in for three months?" Oliver asked.

"Yeah, so far so good. Though my wife and daughters don't like that I'm always away, but they do like the perks," Harry explained.

"They'll get used to it. Speaking of perks, you enjoying the benefits of your position? Hopefully you picked an eager secretary, if you know what I mean."

Harry took a moment to answer. He knew how corrupt some individuals were in his position, but he liked to think of himself as a straight shooter.

"Well, I have a loving wife. I'm a happy family man."

"Well young man, your outlook will change with time."

Both men reached the front of the vibrant hotel. Harry looked up at the towering structure and thought about his daughters. They were suckers for amusement rides, and he knew they would love the attractions that overlooked the entertainment capital of the world.

"Well, Harry. The night is young. Let me introduce you to a friend of mine, she specializes in horizontal entertainment."

Harry pondered the query, being nearly three thousand miles from home certainly made his actions seem disjoint, but then he answered by pulling out his cell phone.

"No, thanks. I'm going to call my wife. It's getting late back in the Northeast," he responded.

"Ah. Okay, but come find me later...if you get hungry," Oliver offered with a murky grin.

With his words, Oliver broke away and walked toward the hotel's entrance. Harry watched the pudgy man shuffle through the crowd and wondered whether the state senator from the South would be so egoistical if he lacked the flashy title.

Harry leaned against a ledge. He had a perfect view of the bustling Las Vegas Strip. Electric lights bathed the night sky. An army of tourists marched like a colony of busy ants.

What an unbelievable sight, he thought as he twirled his wedding ring.

Harry looked down at his cell phone and began to dial his familiar home number, but an odd feeling suddenly overwhelmed him. It was a feeling equivalent to déjà vu, but it lacked a proper label. It was as if his instincts were telling him to turn around. Harry obeyed and spun his body. His focus rushed toward a woman prowling in the pack. She was tall and had long brunette hair, which flowed in the cool desert air. But it was her intriguing outfit that captured the brunt of Harry's attention. She wore tight leopard-patterned pants, which started well beneath her diamond-pierced naval, and a matching top barely covered her plump breasts. She had a confident sway to her step and the leopard spots made her look like the animal she was trying to mimic.

Harry stared at her bare midriff showing a hint of a six-pack, which begged for further inspection. She sauntered his way, and as he glanced up at her face, she stole his gaze with her hunting eyes. The woman stopped several feet from Harry and wielded a cigarette from some unknown location.

"Do you have a light?" she coolly asked the state congressman.

Harry took a moment to respond. He glanced at the cell phone in his hand, and then looked toward the alluring woman. Then, his animal instincts took charge as he buried his cell phone deep into the confines of his pocket.

"I don't smoke," he responded.

"That didn't answer my question."

She moved in front of Harry and sized him up. His body tingled from the burning gaze of her eyes.

"Sorry, I don't have a light," he answered.

"Conference boy, huh? What does that say? Congressman?" she asked, reading his badge.

Harry looked down at his conference pass and removed it from his neck. The public figure knew this was a time where he had to assume the name of "John Doe."

"Uh, yeah," he chuckled, trying to avoid any further inquires.

She slithered closer as the sweet scent of an aroused woman massaged him. He could feel his heart accelerate, and his pupils widen.

The woman leaned in to his ear and whispered, "You want some company tonight, baby? I'm for sale." As Harry's body froze, she gave his earlobe a slight tug with her teeth.

Harry didn't respond. Thoughts of this woman giving in to his every desire filled his mind. *Maybe I should indulge myself. My new salary would surely allow it*, he considered. Just as quickly, however, the muffled screams and laughter from the amusement rides above brought his mind to his daughters.

"What do you say?" she asked, playfully pulling his tie.

"Sure," he mumbled. Harry couldn't believe his mouth had expelled that simple word. It was as if she reined his thoughts like a jockey managing a stud.

"Lead the way," she responded.

Harry's mind suddenly regressed. He tucked the memories of his wife, his daughters, and his career away in a safe, locking it with a key. Then he put the key in a drawer, not opening it until it was unavoidable. This was how he compartmentalized his strenuous life, and it was a required way of thinking when holding such a demanding career.

Harry moved without thought as he walked through the casino and took the elevator to the nineteenth floor. All his focus was on the woman's supple touch as she held his arm. She kneaded his bicep through the linen of his suit as they walked as one.

The sizable suite greeted them with perfection. The maid had performed a fantastic job of transforming the messy room into an organized den. The leopard-clothed siren broke her hold, moved ahead of Harry, and turned to face him. She had an innocent yet promiscuous grin and her eyes burned into him like a stray cat sizing a mouse.

"Honey, what do you want to do?" she murmured.

Harry thought about the money he had brought with him in his wallet. He wasn't planning to gamble over the two-day conference. Harry just wanted to get in, learn a thing or two, and then get back home. However, he was now glad he had made a bank stop on the way to the airport. Harry unearthed his wallet and fanned out ten bills proudly displaying the image of Benjamin Franklin.

"I'm a saleswoman and you just bought my most coveted product for one hour," she said.

Harry laid the wallet on the nearby table. His merchandise didn't waste any time. She pounced on him, pushing his aroused body to the bed. Her force was surprising, but he let her power and conviction devour him. Her lips were warm and moist. He could feel her teeth press against his neck from the thrust of each kiss. She undid his tie and ripped off his shirt. Harry lay back and stared at the painting of a forest hanging on the wall behind the bed. He pictured himself in those woods, pictured two animals succumbing to their primitive instincts. As his eyes rolled back, the woman lapped his chest and abdomen as her paws unfastened his pants. She was a true expert and seemed to understand the fundamental laws of good business—put the customer first.

She threw his pants on the ground, and then went for the last piece of the puzzle, his shorts. Harry closed his eyes as the woman's claws grabbed his cotton boxers. She slid them off his legs and tossed them far away on the other side of the room. As his hormones screamed, Harry felt a tickle on his left hand. Then, she removed her burning body from his.

Harry lay completely naked except for his thin socks. He could feel his heavy breathing vibrating his chest as he yearned for her to engulf him. Harry panted, his mind filling with erotic thoughts of what may come with this woman, but the lack of caress seemed unnaturally long.

Finally, Harry opened his eyes, but the view omitted the enthralling temptress. He looked at the painting on the wall, and then shifted his eyes toward the table near the door. Then he saw the champion saleswoman holding his money-filled wallet, political credentials, and wedding ring.

"All you politicians think with your dicks," she roared in a changed tone. The hunter reached deep within Harry's safe and took his life in her hands. Then like that, she scurried out of the room.

Harry sat up. His instincts prepared him to run after the conniving whore, but his exposed body mocked him. There was no time to dress, as every passing moment provided the leopard a clear escape back into the jungle. Harry suddenly realized the stark truth of his situation, the truth that he had been exploited in the worst possible way. Thoughts of his political demise flashed through his mind, but even more horrifically was the thought of betraying his family.

Harry stared at the plush carpet on the hotel room floor. He tried to find a way to solve his damning conundrum, but every possible solution ended with him losing a part of his professional or personal life.

Why did you do this!? his conscience yelled.

Harry closed his eyes in defeat, but as he opened them, he saw something bizarre. The plush carpet had changed color. Suddenly, the smell of sweat hit his nose. He looked at his chest and saw his conference badge covering the front of his full suit. Then, his eyes shifted to his left ring finger. His wife's offering from their wedding was still there.

Harry looked up and realized he was back at the conference, his coffee in front of him, the gray-haired speaker still babbling.

What happened? he asked himself. Then, Harry concluded he was somehow given a second chance to choose the correct path.

"That wraps up my presentation. Any questions from the audience?" asked the gray-haired man on stage.

The crowd remained mute. Harry saw Oliver Gaspy lock eyes with him. The flustered congressman named Harry sprang from his chair, grabbed his papers, and then scurried out of the conference room. He was the first to reach the cab line, which awarded him with an awaiting taxi.

"The Stratosphere, please," he said to driver.

Harry grabbed his cell phone with his sweaty hands. He dialed his home number without flinching.

"Hello?" his wife answered.

Her soft purr suddenly put Harry's weary mind at ease. The state congressman beamed as he talked.

"Hi honey. I miss you so much. The conference isn't working out and I think I'll take the red-eye home. I love you."

Harry arrived at the entrance to the Stratosphere. While hundreds of people roamed the Las Vegas Strip bathed by the electric lights, Harry didn't look at anyone.

From that day forward, the image of a hungry leopard filled the politician's mind if it ever wandered into the forbidden part of the jungle.

I bet that story applies to a quarter of the male population in this city, probably even more on the weekends. This city rarely gives you a second chance. Harry is lucky.

We're almost there. Doesn't the Strip look so small from this view? You can see from the Mandalay Bay to the Stratosphere in a half turn of the head.

These traffic lights are so long. It gives the mind time to drift, and a drifting mind should *not* be on the road. I see you eyeing those neon lights at that massage parlor. Hey, did you read ahead? Go on. Read the next one. This is one of my very favorites.

The Happy Ending

The road ahead was dark and bare. Michael Thurston loved this part of his drive, the short five miles from his desert home. He was a tall, fit man ripened to the age of forty. Even though Michael was college educated, nothing could beat the freedom of driving a taxi. And what better place to do it than in the entertainment capital of the world, Las Vegas. Working the graveyard shift had its benefits—less traffic, bigger tips, and of course, the interesting characters that roamed the night streets.

As Michael drove, he saw the familiar used car dealer he passed every day. Up ahead on his right was a 24-hour gas station lighting the night sky. Then he saw the "Happy Massage Parlor." It was a small, trite business, nestled between a closed barbershop and psychic, with Asian graphics and writing covering its outside. Michael always wondered what lay beyond that glassless facade. The sign always brightly displayed "Open," but he never saw any cars parked in front.

I have to get one of them happy endings, if they actually exist, he thought. This was one of those stereotypes that mystified him.

Michael always chickened out at the last moment and just kept driving. There was something peculiar about it. *Do people actually go there for a massage?* he asked himself. Nevada law prohibited any sexual acts within the Clark County limits, but everyone knew that illicit activities filled the Vegas underground.

A typical night of work lay ahead for Michael. His fares included the usual drunken college guys shuffling between strip clubs, a few uptight businessmen leaving the convention halls from all-nighters, and several couples heading back to the airport to catch the red-eye. Overall, he made a cool five hundred and twenty two dollars in tips and a ticket to see Bette Midler in concert. Outstanding, except for the Bette Midler ticket. To him, the paper ticket was worth more in burned heat energy than in the show itself.

It was five a.m. and an awesome night's work for the nonchalant cabby. The ride out of the city was always nice, as the quick glimpses in the rear-view provided Michael with a sense of accomplishment. He helped move people to places in the shortest distance and in comfort. Something about a clean cab made his job feel more important. That's why he always vacuumed it before every shift.

Michael stopped the car at a red light. The one thing he noticed about this town was the length of the traffic lights. Red seemed to easily last an extra minute or two than in most other cities, and it took getting used to. Michael knew it was because of a secret agreement between the cab driver union and the city traffic authority, but it was fine by him. It meant a nice ten to fifteen percent gain in cab fare from the longer idling.

Michael glanced around and saw the familiar 24-hour gas station lit up with heavenly lights. Then, like the North Star beckoning in the cloudless sky, he saw the glaring "Open" sign in front of the "Happy Massage Parlor." Thoughts of intrigue raced through his mind. *Maybe I should treat myself?* he pondered.

The light turned green and Michael accelerated, but his hands did something strange. They turned into the parking lot of the massage parlor almost as if they had a mind of their own, telling his brain to go for it.

Michael parked and stepped out into the deserted lot. He felt a slight hint of sleaziness overwhelm him, but intrigue far outweighed it. He staggered toward the ominous door, clumping on the hard ground.

Michael pushed the door, but it didn't budge. He wondered whether they were closed. But the sign that read "Pull" explained the situation vividly. He entered as his nostrils immediately received the concocted smell of strange oils and mothballs. The back of the "Open" sign was the only light, which consumed the entryway in radiating red. The cones of Michael's eyes took a moment to adjust. Asian words painted the wall and an abused vinyl couch stood in the corner. As Michael scanned the entryway, he didn't hear that someone actually slid in front of him. The weary-eyed Asian hostess looked about fifty, but it was hard to tell, as Asians seemed to hide their age well.

"Hello. You come for massage?" she murmured in a broken accent.

"Uh...yeah," Michael replied.

"What type of girl you want?"

He didn't know how to respond. The question caught him off guard.

"An Asian one," he joked.

The comment didn't seem to faze the woman. Sarcasm with the English language probably wasn't something she mastered.

"Sixty dollar, plus tip to girl. She make you feel real good... Pay now."

"Pay now?" he asked.

"Yes. Sixty dollar. Good massage."

Michael opened his bulging wallet in front of her and withdrew exactly sixty dollars from his tips.

She smiled. "Now follow me."

She led him to a door at the end of the shadowy hallway. As she opened it, all that greeted him was a black void. The Asian hostess entered and flipped a switch igniting a small pink lamp shaped like a woman's corset.

"Here you go. Take clothes off. Girl will come inside. Three minute," she blankly instructed.

He paused, unable to speak, and simply gave her an acknowledging nod. The contents of the room hypnotized him. Across from the door sat a small cart on wheels covered with half-filled bottles of lotions and oils. A battered massage table stood directly in the center of the room with a sheet covering it like the main prop on stage in a magic show. What stirred Michael the most was the objects hanging on the wall—weapons directly out of a Kung Fu movie! A set of nunchucks, three samurai swords, and a shiny pair of handcuffs were prominently displayed. As he contemplated them, curious to their involvement in a massage, he realized he used most of his three minutes.

Michael began to disrobe, but the moment he kicked his pants off, the door opened. He turned his head and his eyes locked with a cute Asian girl dressed only in a silky black kimono. She barely looked twenty and her slanted eyes and alluring smile immediately perked his attention.

"You want massage? My name Gee-Gee."

Michael was nervous. Even though he had seen his share of women over the years, especially during college, something about this girl was different. He felt like an adolescent in junior high out on a first date.

"Yeah. Massage is good," he simply replied.

She glanced down at his boxers and socks still doing their job on his pale body.

"Everything off," she commanded.

"Oh, okay," he gingerly responded.

She walked over to the corner of the room to grab a towel, which removed her gaze from him. Michael felt weird getting fully nude in the same room with this girl. *Is this normal?* he thought. *When is she going to ask me if I want sex?*

Michael obeyed her simple commands. He dropped his cotton-white Hanes exposing himself to the musty air in the room. Finally, he pinched his socks off and placed them on his pile of clothes. Michael stepped onto the cold concrete floor. He paused for a moment fully naked from head to toe savoring the rather strange situation. Just ten minutes ago, he was ending his shift from a typical night in Sin City. But now, he was standing undressed with some Asian girl named Gee-

Gee who was probably half his age and seemed to barely speak his language.

Swiftly, Michael slid under the towel, face up. He stared at the faded dragons painted on the ceiling. He thought about how many other lonely travelers saw this same image, awaiting their fate.

"No... Over... I work back first," she murmured.

Gee-Gee picked up the towel as Michael flipped over. He positioned his head into a circular pillow open in the middle just enough for his eyes to peer through.

Michael watched her dainty little toes shuffle around on the floor. Her nails were polished in a dark shade of red and one of her left toes had a small silver ring on it. He focused on the ring until his attention shifted to the skin of his back.

Her touch was warm and sensual. She kneaded her paws back and forth over his aching muscles like a kitten preparing for dinner. The years of sitting on his foam-padded car seat seemed to wither away with each pass of her hands. She was quiet, which surprised Michael. He waited for her elastic voice to whisper in his ear, "You want happy ending?" or "Will massage all over for more money." But he heard nothing, just the cute little grunts of her enthusiastic work.

Then in a sudden motion, her hands left his back. He suddenly felt cold and alone craving her dainty hands to return. Michael thought of the experience thus far and was shocked for not indulging himself sooner.

His wandering mind quickly returned to the girl as her delicate feet came back into his view. But what he felt next was unexpected, even downright bizarre. He felt his wrists squeeze together and heard the click of something metallic.

What the hell is going on? he wondered. Michael attempted to move his hands free, but they didn't cooperate. Something was holding them together behind his back. Then he remembered the handcuffs on the wall.

"I didn't sign up for this!" he yelled.

But his exclamation went unanswered.

Michael did his best to sit up, but he soon realized the Asian girl was nowhere to be found. What he did see, however, shocked him; it made him tremble. A burly middle-aged Asian man exploded through the door. He had a look of rage as he muscled toward Michael.

Terrified, Michael rolled off the edge of the table and jumped to his feet. The fact he was stark naked had no effect on him. Michael cared more about avoiding the wrath of this irate man than the embarrassment of a clothesless body.

Michael shuffled around the table dodging the thug, but as he moved, Gee-Gee scurried back in. She had no interest in the scuffle; she went right for his stack of clothes. Her hands reached deep inside his pants pockets. Michael quickly recognized the focus of this bizarre situation. It was his wallet, and it was now firmly grasped in Gee-Gee's hands.

Michael thought of his five hundred and twenty two dollars, minus sixty, he had stashed in there. She could have the Bette Midler ticket, but he knew she could probably care even less about that than he did.

Michael had to think fast as the muscleman failed to relinquish his fury. Gee-Gee ran out leaving the two men to battle inside the dank room.

Michael kicked the cart filled with the massage oils. They spilled over the robust ground. He glanced at the samurai swords, but realized that with no hands free, he couldn't remove them from the wall. Then in a blur, the large Asian's feet slipped out from under him. His 300-pound frame plummeted toward the hard concrete floor. Michael watched in shock, and then waited for his attacker to rise back up.

Abruptly, the burly man stood with a look of rage on his face, a look that terrified Michael. The middle-aged cab driver realized he had just doused the already blazing fire with a bucket of gasoline. The Asian thug hurled the cart back at him. Michael ducked as the metal pounded the wall and dislodged one of the samurai swords from its spot on display. Michael watched as the razor-sharp weapon wobbled above his head, and then slipped from its brace. He tried to avoid the blade as he arched his back struggling to protect his head and vital organs. But before he knew it, the metal clanked on the ground and he saw something fly in the air. Both men suddenly stopped cold realizing the jagged consequences of their brawl.

The Asian man was speechless. He knew he was only instructed to jolt the customers and throw them out the back door with a good scare, but he had one who was actually willing to fight back.

Michael felt his adrenaline subside as a bizarre tingle overwhelmed his crotch. It was a sensation he had never felt before. Suddenly, his eyes shifted to something rolling on the ground. He blinked a few times trying to focus. At first, he thought it was a bottle of the slippery lotion, but he quickly realized it was in the shape of a penis. Michael looked down at his groin and saw a bloody hole where his manhood had once occupied, the color red seeping down his leg. A bolt of lightning traversed through the forty-year-old cab driver. He could not think. He could not feel. He could only...run.

Michael bolted from the room.

"You damn chinks! You cut my dick off!" he screamed.

He reached the lobby only to find his masseuse and the Asian hostess counting money, *his* money, under the bright red light. Both women whipped their heads around at the sight of Michael's naked body. Then in a flash, Gee-Gee grabbed the money-filled wallet and thrust her way outside.

Michael looked at the venomous masseuse, as he wanted nothing more than to beat the hell out of her. Even though he had no idea how he was going to do it, he had to catch her.

The hostess watched in utter shock at the naked man scurrying like a chicken with its head cut off, or more specifically, his *dick*. She looked down and saw the blood oozing from the void in Michael's groin. This was a customer unlike any other.

Michael used his hip to burst open the door. The cool brisk air of morning greeted his body. It didn't seem that cold when he walked in, but then again, he was fully nude right now and filled with excruciating pain.

Up ahead, Gee-Gee dashed through the parking lot. Michael hustled toward her, hands still cuffed behind his back. He could feel the shards of debris from the asphalt stick to his callused feet, but that didn't stop his drive. He passed his cab, which was placidly parked in the same spot.

"Get back here!" he yelled.

Gee-Gee darted into the street at full force. A car's blaring horn didn't deter her as she continued plowing forward. Michael followed her lead and ran across the street, blood covering his legs as if he had a leaking catheter. Inside the car, a retired man driving for the morning newspaper received an eyeful he sure wasn't expecting. "Only in Vegas," he mouthed to himself.

As Michael ran, thoughts of his penis rolling around on the filthy floor filled his mind. Maybe he should have stayed behind and begged for an ambulance rather than running naked at five in the morning through the bowels of Las Vegas. But all he could focus on was the Asian girl's black kimono flapping in the dry desert air from her cat-like speed.

The 24-hour gas station filled the sunless sky with light as the masseuse ran toward it. But as fate would have it, a police officer on foot saw the ensuing commotion.

The officer took a moment to assess the bizarre situation, but he did what his training had taught him. Draw your weapon, neutralize the scene, and then ask questions.

"Freeze!" he blurted.

Gee-Gee stopped cold in her tracks.

"Down on the ground, both of you!" the officer commanded.

Michael followed and laid on the chilly ground resembling his pose on the massage table, except this time he didn't have a nice pillow for his head.

The officer saw Michael's hands cuffed together resting on his tan-less butt cheeks as blood pooled on the ground beneath him.

"My dick! They cut off my dick!" Michael exclaimed as the officer looked at Gee-Gee.

Then the cab driver's body, and his mind, gave up. Michael passed out.

Later in the morning, Michael woke up in a hospital bed with thick gauze bandaging his groin. The paramedics had recovered his lost penis and surgeons had sewed it back on without any problems. Aside from a scar at the sliced point, he would regain full use of his little head. Apparently, the penis could be left severed for a few hours under the right conditions and still be successfully reattached. Fortunately for Michael, he made it in time.

The recuperating cab driver also got his money back, including the sixty dollars, and reclaimed his abandoned clothes that had once covered his body. The police immediately revoked the business license of the "Happy Massage Parlor," and the Asian culprits were apprehended.

As Michael recovered in his hospital bed, he glanced at the souvenir handcuffs lying next to him on his nightstand and thought, *Next time, just keep driving.*

Ouch! Caveat emptor...

Well, we're here at the office. This place is strange. Our bosses are all Israeli businessmen driving German-made cars. How are they making that kind of money—selling T-shirts and souvenirs on the Strip? What did we sell tonight? Two hundred bucks. It just doesn't add up. Wait. Let's see what this Mercedes is doing. What is that on the roof? It's a mattress. Hey, there's Amit. See, I knew these guys are up to something. Look at the four of them pile out and bring that mattress through the back door. What is that for?

I'll just run this in myself. Stay here and keep an eye out for any more suspicious activity. You might as well read another story.

A Dance to Remember

This straw is too long. Why do they have to give you a long straw with a small drink? They should make two sizes. This looks stupid. What is that wind noise? Did I leave the back door open? The dash light would be on if I'd left it open. But maybe this car doesn't have that option? This was the cheapest car on the lot. Why would it have a dash light? That noise is getting louder. Is the door going to open? Why do they make car doors with two latches? It should either be open or closed. There shouldn't be a half-open. Why am I even going to this thing? I never go to these things. Am I even going in the right direction? Where is this house? Did I pass it? Wait... Is that it? Yes. Number 529. Wow. It's much bigger than I expected.

I park my compact car between a BMW and a Lexus. I open the door, but wait as I hear a woman's voice. I figure I will let her pass. I hate meeting new people. Why did I agree to come? I'll just hang out at the bar. The voice I hear is from a woman walking in with her date. That dress shows her big ass. Why would she wear that? I bet it's him. Yeah. He looks like an ass man. I could never wear that. I wonder how my ass would look. I hope this green thing I'm wearing is okay. Geez, my boobs are too small. I'm never going to meet a guy in there with these things.

The cool night air hits me. I walk a few feet, but then realize I forgot the gift. How dumb am I? Finally, I drift toward the door like a stray cat lured by the lights. I can hear laughing inside. Am I going to be okay? I keep moving, and then finally press the doorbell. The seconds seem like minutes. Then, the door opens, the warmth from inside mollifying me.

"Sofia. You made it!" Michelle says.

"Please come in," David goes.

I smile and step inside. I give Michelle a hug. Aw... It feels like we're kids again. I'm so glad I came. David gives me a kiss on the cheek. He is such a nice guy. Michelle is a lucky girl. Why can't I find a guy like him? I give her the card and the bottle of wine.

"Thank you so much!" Michelle says.

"Excellent. Merlot, my favorite," David goes.

"I don't know how long I'll stay," I say.

"Well, I'm glad you made it. This party wouldn't be complete without my..." Michelle stumbles.

"Ha! What exactly are we?" I add.

"Yeah, how did you girls meet?" David says.

"Elementary school," we both say at the same time.

"You're my longest friend," Michelle adds.

"Even longer than me?" David says as he leans in and sneaks a kiss from his fiancée.

"Yes, even longer than you, honey," Michelle says.

I can't look. It's as if I'm not even here. Wow, there are a lot of people at this party.

"Well, enjoy yourself. We have a special treat for everyone," Michelle finally says.

"Get a drink. It's an open bar," David adds.

My tail goes up like a cat hearing the garage door open.

"That sounds like a great idea," I say.

I step past the entryway. Michelle taps my shoulder.

"Don't be shy. There are some single men lurking around," she whispers, batting her eyes.

I grin, and then meander into the Great Room. I step into the busiest place, yet it feels the loneliest. Girls giggle. Guys clank wine glasses. Couples mingle. I sweep the room with my eyes, looking for someone I know or someone who knows me, but it's as if I am invisible. The place looks like a young philanthropist's mixer. The problem is I don't even know what that big word means.

A grand piano sits across the dance floor. Wow, that's a beautiful piano. Ah... I finally see someone calling my name—the bar. As I prepare to move, a clap fills the room and slaps my ears.

"If I could have your attention for just a moment," David announces to the crowd.

The chattering dies down. Everyone turns. I wish I could do that, declare my desire for a date. But would anyone listen to me?

"Michelle and I would like to thank all of you for coming to our engagement party and for your gracious gifts. As promised, we have a very special guest for you tonight."

The participants lift their heads. I too look around. Do these people know George Clooney? As babble fills the crowd, a man in his fifties steps next to David. He wears a polished tuxedo, which makes him look like a doorman at the Waldorf. Who the hell is that? But then it clicks. He's a pianist.

"The famous Pianist Mister Richard Hayworth will provide you with his beautiful music this evening," David adds.

Gasps pour from the crowd as applause follows. I don't know much about classical music, but then again, maybe my future husband in the crowd will teach me. I clap too.

"Mister Hayworth has played for many celebrities and had audiences everywhere from on the Las Vegas Strip to the White House for the past four Presidents. Without further ado, I present to you, Mister Hayworth."

The crowd silences and steps off the dance floor. All I can do is watch as the pianist glides. His tail reaches past his knees. Why do they make tails? It looks silly, but this guy appears to be able to pull it off. Who is this guy anyway? I should Google him. I wonder if he is single.

He sits with perfect posture. Ah... So that's why he wears a tail. It flows over the back. Very nice. The pianist raises his hand. I hold my breath. Then, he lunges at the keys. A gentle song pours from the piano. I never heard it before, yet it seems vaguely familiar. Two flowing bodies enter my view. It's David and Michelle dancing on the floor. Aw... They are so cute. I'm jealous. Look at how he holds her. He has big hands. I like a man with big hands, but not too big. This party is just so nice. More couples join them. I want to dance. Someone ask me. I see a clean-cut guy with slicked hair. He is nice. Is he coming this way? Did he see me staring? What should I do? Oh, there's his girlfriend. That bitch! Where is the bar?

I dance my way to the lonely bar. A female bartender smiles at me. Geez. I can't even get a grubby guy to flirt with. Why is she wearing a tuxedo? Especially with a cummerbund. What woman wears a tuxedo? But as I near her and see her smile grow, I realize what type of woman wears a tuxedo.

"That's a nice green dress," she says.

I can tell she's staring at my boobs. What should I say in return? *Nice suit.* This is weird.

"Thank you," I finally say.

"What can I get you, dear?" she asks.

I eye some wine, but this is an open bar. I shift my eyes higher and see the harder stuff.

"Uh. Something strong," I admit.

She grabs a bottle of gin from the middle shelf.

"Stronger."

Her hand moves up a shelf to a bottle of brandy.

"Keep going," I continue.

She rests her hand on a black and white label—"Jack Daniel's Old Tennessee Whiskey." I nod.

"On the rocks," I add.

She scoops some ice into a glass. I grip it, my stubby nails on display. The bartender opens the pristine bottle and pauses.

"You sure this is what you want?" she asks.

I nod again like in some old western movie. But I can't figure out who the cowboy is.

The alcohol devours the ice. I grab the glass and swirl the liquid. The cubes cry. Then, I take a sip. Wow. That's damn strong. Did she just see me wince? I'm sure she did, but I hope no one else did.

"Good luck," the bartender goes.

I roll my eyes and move away from the bar, away from her. I amble to the dance floor and take another taste. This time it's not as bad. Couples dance to another moving song. That pianist is good. I take a larger gulp now. I hate this place. What am I doing here? I should go. These guys aren't for me. They want a Stepford wife, not a girl who works at the bookstore. I couldn't play a Stepford wife. There's no way I could handle the other wives. I know I would beat someone up. My mind says I should go, but my body takes another drink of the booze, and then another.

I feel weird. I'm going to go, but let me finish this drink first. This tastes strange. Maybe that bartender put something in it. I bet she wants me out of this green dress. But she opened the bottle in front of me. Wow. These people are really dancing. Dance, dance. That dress flows. I feel odd. The room is spinning. That music is loud. People are everywhere. I'm going to be sick. I put my hand on my forehead. The glass falls to the floor. Did someone turn off the lights?

Silence surrounds me. I see the color black. I'm in a room. I know that, but the lights are out. Maybe my eyes are closed. I use all of my energy to open them. Then, the lights ignite.

I am on the floor. I stand up and realize that I am still in the Great Room. But, where are all the people? The void of the thirty-foot-tall room encircles me, no music, no pianists, no bartender—nobody. What happened?

"Hello, my dear," a masculine voice says, gripping my mind.

I spin to find the voice, to find the man. A shadow enters my view. I raise my head and see black dress shoes at the base of a dark suit. I follow the pin stripes up to the handsome face of a man in his thirties. He exudes confidence as his arresting eyes pierce me.

"Where is everyone? What happened?" I question.

He offers his masculine hand. I place mine inside as it melts.

"Would you like to dance?" he asks, bringing me to my feet.

"But there's no music."

"There will be," he says, gesturing to my side.

A cool pianist stands near his instrument. He is a different man from the one I remember, different by his white hair and white suit. He bows graciously, and then assumes his position, his white tail draping behind him. He caresses the keys. A soft rhythm flows over me.

The handsome man in front of me extends his hand. I am nervous. Dancing is something I like to watch, but actually dancing on this huge floor—nope. He smiles. Damn, he's so cute. I don't even know his name.

"It's just me and you," he says.

I study his sturdy hand, but as I slowly accept it, his other arm sweeps me off my feet. We move to the music. What step is this? I don't know any steps. As my mind races, I feel his firm grasp around my waist. Just when I don't know whether to go left or right, his hand moves me in the direction. This is nice. He is leading me. Just go with it. Whoa. There is a twirl. I laugh as he chuckles. His eyes are so green.

We move as one. Just him being there, guiding me, twirling me, dipping me, sets my mind at ease. If Michelle could only see me now. Where is she? Where is everyone? Ah... I should stop thinking.

I'm really dancing. I love this. I love this man. I get brave. We twirl the other way. Then, we break our hold as I keep winding. Wow. I'm really spinning. I feel so free. I stop, but then suddenly the music stops too. I look at the pianist, but the shiny black piano sits alone. I look for my prince, but he is gone. Oh no. What happened? The room seems strange. Are the walls moving? Wow. I feel weird again. The room is spinning. Then in a pop, the lights go out.

Darkness fills my view. Where am I? Is this a dream? I hear the sound of someone yelling. It's loud yet it's not. It's as if I'm underwater. Lights come on. Everything is out of focus. Faces tower over me.

"Is she alright? She needs air," I hear from the crowd.

David pushes through. He kneels.

"Sofia, are you okay?" he asks.

Finally, everything comes back. My head really hurts. David helps me sit up. People back up. What happened? Someone picks up a fallen glass next to me. Oh, that drink. Now I remember. But I want to go back to the dream.

"Did you hurt yourself?" David continues.

"Uh. No. I just had too much to drink," I say, clutching my head.

"Can you stand?"

"I think so."

David helps me up. My legs feel okay. Wow. Did I just pass out? I feel so embarrassed.

"What were you drinking?" David asks.

I see the bartender looking overhead. I turn to David.

"Something way too strong."

"Do you need us to call an ambulance?"

"No. No. It's okay," I insist.

The crowd backs up. My cheeks turn red. I can't look at these people. They probably think I'm a dork. Something white catches my eye. It's the white from a man's suit jacket. I look at his face. His clean shave and styled hair look bizarrely familiar. He grabs me with his eyes—his green eyes. It's him!

"I'm fine now," I mutter, lost in the handsome man's gaze.

"Okay, everyone. She's fine. Please continue your fun," David declares to the crowd.

The people disperse. I look at David, but keep the color white in my peripheral vision.

"Thank you so much, David," I say.

"You're welcome, Sofia," he replies as Michelle runs to his side.

"Sofia. Someone said you fainted. Are you okay?" Michelle says from my side.

I turn to her and wink as the handsome man approaches me. I look at him, and he smiles.

"Hello, my dear," he says with that unforgettable voice.

He says it with a grin, as if he too knows about my dream—our dream. I blush. The sound of beauty massages my ears as the pianist plays. The crowd re-engages. I realize that I'm in the middle of the dance floor.

"I was going to ask you to dance, but are you okay after your fall?" he asks.

"I'm fine...really. And I would love to dance," I reply.

He offers his hand, and I accept it. Then, he scoops me up, and we move as one. Gone are my worries, my anxieties over a place that I had once felt lost in. All that I care about is this moment—this moment lost in a dance that I'll always remember.

Unknown parking lot behind the Strip
12:39 a.m.

I'm back. Anything going down? What did you think of the story? I always liked that one. I can relate to it. I wonder when I'll wake up.

The office always freaks me out. I made no eye contact in there. Let's blow this joint. We have another twenty-minute drive, and then the real party starts. Don't worry. This gig will be fun. No, I'm not a call girl, well, maybe in a twisted sort of way. Trust me. I'll introduce you to some cool cats. I wish I knew these guys before I moved here. Do you see those lights and those people on the Strip? Well, we're heading in the opposite direction—into the void of the night.

Read another story and enjoy the ride.

Scorched

Sunlight bathed a lush landscape. The color green sprawled across a mountainside. Trees reached for the blue sky. A man in his thirties stood with a notepad and pencil. He wore a scorched white uniform covered with black soot. A backpack was slung over his shoulder. His name badge barely read "Anderson." He appeared fit and healthy like a man who worked out at night instead of ate out. While grit covered his face and short brown hair, his handsome qualities still shined through. In fact, some women may have found him more attractive now than if he were all cleaned up.

Anderson grabbed a hanging tree branch with his gloved hand. He analyzed the leaf. Unusual swirls covered the green plant, swirls representing its complex system of veins. He followed the pattern with his finger, and then drew the same design in his notepad.

Water vapor danced across a football-sized pond. Stillness filled the water as if it were a sheet a glass reflecting the surrounding trees. A speck of white shifted. It was Anderson trekking along the gravelly edge of the water. His burned boots crunched on the ground with each step. Anderson stopped, kneeled on the bank, and then reached for the water. He moved slowly. His finger pierced the liquid and sent a ripple across the pond. Anderson removed his hand, and then unfastened his glove. His exposed hand moved toward the water. Finally, his pointer finger grazed the liquid. He held it for a moment, and then recoiled it quickly. Anderson dabbed a droplet on his tongue. He licked, but then coughed and spit. Anderson wrote in his notepad, "Water is horribly salty."

The wandering man continued down the shoreline. He gravitated toward a rock formation. As he approached, he noticed rocks colored in brown, dark green, gray, and red, which embodied the shape of something similar to Stonehenge. Anderson paused and swept his eyes across the landscape. Plants flourished with life, yet Anderson's location seemed lifeless.

Anderson continued his exploration. He came across a large boulder field extending for miles. He hopped across each rock like a kid playing a game. The only problem was that Anderson had already forgotten his childhood. He stopped for a moment and filled his eyes with the open space.

"Hello! Anyone out there!?" he yelled, but the sound of silence replied.

Anderson continued his journey. He jumped from one boulder to another. Finally, he reached an area with smaller rocks. He picked up the pace, his movements quick and exact.

He saw the distant dense forest. Anderson looked down. The color brown was everywhere. Rock after rock rolled over him. But then, the color red struck the cones of his eyes. Anderson stopped cold. It was a dazzling red flower. He squatted and saw the vivid red blossom connecting to a brown stalk. Anderson caressed the flower as if it were his wife's breast. Swirls in the shape of horseshoes painted each petal. Anderson sketched the pattern in his notepad.

Satisfied with his artwork, Anderson put his notepad and pencil away in his pack. Then, he gripped the flower and broke it free from its food supply. Suddenly, the severed stalk oozed a brown liquid and gurgled to its death. Anderson jumped back. He glanced at the radiant red flower in his hand, but it too had lost its life, now the color of unconscious gray.

Anderson's eyes squinted with curiosity. He laid the dead flower on the ground, and then rooted inside his bag. He unearthed a Zippo lighter covered with the image of two dice. Anderson flicked it. A flame eight inches high danced on the wick. He brought the fire to the broken stalk. It ignited into an inferno. Just as fast, the fire extinguished removing the stalk like a Vegas magic act. Anderson put the lighter in his back pocket, and then removed his notepad. He wrote below his drawing of the horseshoe flower, "High reaction to fire."

Later, Anderson hiked through the dense forest. Green consumed his eyes, but the color red rested in the middle of his view, the color red from a boulder. Anderson reached the rock, and then propped up against it. Inside his notepad, he studied a hand drawn map with labels, "Rock Field," "Pond," and "Hill." At the bottom of the page, the word "Base" was labeled in a circle. Its markings appeared darker and heavier than the other drawings. It looked as if a stressed man, a man at the start of a daunting mission, had drawn it. Anderson sketched another symbol on the top of the page and labeled it "Large Red Boulder."

A cool breeze flowed through the area rustling the leaves on the trees. Anderson felt the cold wrap his face, and then enter through the crease in his collar, chilling his skin. He could do only one thing—keep moving. As Anderson stepped past the large rock, he froze. Something caught his eye, something that was bizarrely out-of-place, yet was real enough to shiver his bones. It was a grave.

Anderson saw a mound of rocks with a cross made from branches. His heart pounded and his mind filled with fear, but he thought about his mission, the only mission that he knew. Anderson checked the cross. A date was carved in the wood, "4209 – 4102." He furrowed his brow as questions ran through his mind. He searched for a name of the fallen victim carved in the wood, but as he did, the sound of a squeal hit his ears. It was a sound unlike anything that had ever entered the ears of the thirty-year-old man. Anderson's mind stopped, his muscles clenched, but his heart rate increased.

Stillness filled the forest. Anderson's eyes widened and his ears opened. At first, he thought his mind had concocted the sound, a trick from being isolated. But then, the sound cut through him again, a sound that scared him beyond belief. Anderson heard trees breaking behind him. A creature was running his way! Turning around was an option, but it was the last option Anderson wanted to take. He darted through the forest. His lungs gasped for oxygen; his steps were erratic. The petrified man cut through the trees. As he ran, he heard the squeal gain strength behind him. He jumped over a rock, moved between trees, and then dashed around a boulder. Precision timed each movement, but precise also described the creature behind him.

Anderson expelled from the dense woods like a piece of meat coughed up by the Heimlich Maneuver. He reached a grassy hill. He ran up, fueled by adrenaline. His muscles flexed as his boots dug into the muddy ground. The bag on his shoulder flopped left and right with each movement of his unsteady body. The top of the hill was just steps away. Anderson used all of his energy to reach it. His legs stretched one last time. But as he arrived at the crest, his momentum propelled him through the air and down the other side. Anderson's body bashed against the muddy grass. His pack flew from his back. He flipped over and over like a kid amusing his friends after school. But for Anderson, his friend was already amused.

Anderson finally ground to a halt at the bottom of the hill, mud covering his body. He stared at the spinning blue sky. His mind had lost its way, rattled from a dozen flips in the air. But then, his mind regained focus and thought of one thing—the monster.

Anderson sat up as his eyes adjusted from the fall. He tried to stand, but his beaten body only mocked him. Suddenly, the cry of his stalker penetrated him. Anderson felt for his pack, but it was too far away. All the lost man could do was hold his legs and lower his head. He regressed to an infant as he prepared to meet his shadow. He didn't, in fact he couldn't, face the creature. All he focused on was the dot of light that he saw as he clenched his eyelids closed. He thought about his son, his wife, and his life. But as he centered on the memory of his family forever burned into his mind, the sound of hisses and ticks stole the light away.

Anderson could feel the creature's hot breath on his neck. The smell of the beast hit him. It was like a mix of burnt rubber and plastic. Anderson held his breath as he prepared to leave to go to the place beyond. But then, something entered his mind—the image of fire. Acting without sight, he reached into his back pocket and felt the sturdy metal casing of his lighter. Anderson exposed it to the air, and then flicked it. Even without seeing it, he knew the robust item would light on the first try, just as it did for the past ten years. He held the flame out. He could hear the creature sniffing. Then, the sound of sizzling hit Anderson's ears followed by yelps of pain. Just as fast, Anderson heard the sound of the creature scurrying away. He held his pose as silence finally encircled him. Holding his breath, he opened his eyes, his pupils sucking in light. The color green surrounded him. He was free, given a second chance. But then, he saw something that made his body return to the state that he had just evaded—a three-toed footprint of his stalker easily 12 inches in length.

Numbness plugged Anderson's senses. He swallowed, clutching the metal lighter. Anderson saw his pack some ten feet away. He grabbed it, brushed off the debris, and then grabbed his notepad and pencil. He walked toward the ground where the weight of the unknown creature had pummeled. The artist was forced to sketch it much more quickly than his other drawings. His hand shook, skewing the arcs of each toe. While the footprint was a foot in length, Anderson only had six inches of space. As he finished, he drew a big question mark underneath.

Later, the sun set over the distant mountain. The wind had picked up, rustling the trees. Under the sun, Anderson hustled. He moved with conviction, his steps motivated not by curiosity, but fear.

As the mountain finally blocked the setting sun, Anderson reached the top of a small hill. He studied his notepad. Anderson eyed the word "Hill." Then, he dragged his pointer finger down to the circle labeled "Base." He looked in the direction that his makeshift map had denoted and saw a white object some half-mile away. Anderson licked his lips, and then ran toward the dot.

As twilight remained in the sky, a creature stomped toward a tent. The animal had wide eyes, hungry teeth, and a pounding heart. It was just over six feet tall and wore a layer of artificial skin labeled with eight letters of the English alphabet—"Anderson." The suited man stopped ten feet from the tent. The huffs from his lungs filled the silence as Anderson watched…waited.

"Hello," he finally said.

Only the soft motion of a nearby tree replied. He stepped closer to the tent, his boots crunching on the gravel. Anderson moved the opening aside and saw two sleeping bags. He stood tall and looked beyond the tent at a damaged spacecraft. The ship appeared like a small commuter jet outfitted with a perfectly spherical nose. Its wings were busted, a black mess of soot left behind. But one thing on the craft was not damaged. In fact, it remained flawless like the day it was etched into the ship's polymers. It had 13 red and white stripes and a blue rectangle bearing 51 five-pointed stars; it was the American flag.

Suddenly, the sound of moving gravel hit his ears. Anderson tightened his grip on the lighter as he whipped around. He saw an animal not of this planet, but of the planet

Earth. The image of a beautiful woman scorched by a crash landing filled his eyes. She had the same look in her green eyes that filled Anderson's, the same look shared only by a fallen partner. Her name badge too was damaged, but Anderson didn't need the label to acknowledge her.

"Everett. God...I'm glad it's you. Did you find anything?" Anderson asked.

"I tracked the north side all day... Nothing. I don't know where we are," she said, clutching her pack.

"I found something," he replied with a quiver in his voice.

Anderson removed his notepad from his pack. He opened the most crumpled page, and showed Everett the image sketched with graphite. She shrieked at the sight of the footprint made by some unknown three-toed monster. Tears filled her eyes. While Anderson was lost on a distant planet, uncharted by his country's scientists, he knew that he was all that his partner had left. All he could do was hold on to her and never let go. The two American astronauts embraced under the night sky filled with three moons.

Oh, man. Don't open your eyes! Don't open your eyes! I don't envy them. I wonder whether that planet has its own version of Vegas.

While you were reading, we got a little lost. I know, I know. Don't worry. I will find this place. I've been here so many times you'd think that I would know it by heart. I know there are no lights out here. We are a long way from the lights.

Well, there is one more story left, but I don't know if you should read it. This one is the most twisted yet. I actually wrote this story myself. They say to write what you know...so I did. This one is based on a true story. Go on and read it. I'll make sure you finish it before you meet my friends.

Fresh Blood

Traffic flowed through streets like blood through veins. Casino lights electrified the night sky. Thousands of creatures roamed Fremont Street. An elderly man with a camera held a Las Vegas map. A bum clutched a change cup. Drunks dressed as clowns erupted from a cab. A sexy angel hollered.

A white rental car cut through traffic. A man dressed as Frankenstein stepped into the street. The car slammed on its brakes as the monster crossed the road. Then, the car's engine roared. The rental car accelerated to pass a cab, but the taxi rocketed in front. Five college-aged zombies stumbled on the sidewalk. The rental car slowed.

Two businessmen commanded the car. They were in their mid-thirties, an age when hair clogged the drain of their shower. Both men wore sleek suits wrinkled from a cross-country flight. The man driving was Stephen Henry, a stockbroker who only took chances with other people's money. Barry Mann navigated. He was a sneaky financial analyst who cared more about the Dogs of the Dow than the dogs of his family.

"These idiots! We'd better find another way," Barry blasted.

"Let's just stay on the main road," Stephen cautioned.

"We don't need a vehicular manslaughter on the company's insurance! These drunks are everywhere."

Stephen diverted onto a downtown road. Lifeless casinos filled their view as the car sped away from the lights. Suddenly, the rental bucked.

"This piece of shit," Barry barked as smoke billowed from the hood.

"I got to pull it over."

Stephen steered the dying vehicle onto the side of the comatose street. The car sputtered, and then the engine cut out.

"We'll have to call the rental company," Stephen said.

"It's the middle of the night. The thing's probably just overheating."

They stepped from the car as the cool desert air covered them. Barry scurried to the front and unlatched the hood. Smoke erupted from the puny four-cylinder engine.

"Go get two bottles of water from the trunk," Barry said.

Stephen obeyed. He popped the trunk and opened his briefcase. Convention pamphlets poured out as he rooted for two bottles of water.

Barry tapped the radiator cap with his bare hand.

"Is that smart?" Stephen asked, returning.

Barry gripped the cap, but whipped his hand back. "Damn!"

He tried from a different angle, but the smoking engine only mocked him.

"It needs a rest before we can add it," Barry finally said.

"Well, I don't want to sit out here in the dark."

Both men looked around. Graffiti was painted on a brick building. A bar stood closed with the letter "b" nearly faded away. Boards covered a pawnshop. The street appeared dead as if some plague had stolen its life away. But as the businessmen swept their eyes across the street, one building stood out. It too was dilapidated, but electricity energized its lights. While nearly half of the bulbs were burned out, there were just enough of them to form its signal in the night— Gentlemen's Club. Barry and Stephen looked at each other with a smirk.

Black lights pulsated around the dark club. Heavy metal music wailed. A flexible girl wearing only devil horns twirled on a pole as the lights bathed her porcelain skin. A few weary travelers sprinkled the chairs mesmerized by her hardened nipples.

An area of plush chairs overlooked the action. "VIP Lounge" was marked above the entryway. A pair of sultry legs, wrapped by fishnet stockings, rested against the supple black leather of the best seat in the house. A robe enveloped the venomous vixen. Her nails were painted black, as was her hair. Sex appeal oozed from her aura, but class dominated it. She watched the entire club from her perch. Her name was Catalina.

In a shadowy side of the VIP Lounge, a tiny girl barely 100 pounds soaking wet, grinded on a burly man's groin. Her springy C-cup bounced with the beat of the music. The husky man watched her like a priest watching the communion cup.

"Very nice," the burly man said. "And how old is a sweet thing like you?"

"Eighty-Five."

"Eighty-Five? Come on, sweetie," he joked as he placed his calloused hands on her silky legs. "Have you ever had an older, more experienced man?"

She slowed her motion as the man intensified his. Swiftly, he grabbed her breasts. The girl tried to resist.

Catalina lifted her head like a cat hearing a mouse in the attic. She turned and focused on the burly man ravishing one of her girls. Catalina rose and snaked toward the gormandizing customer.

The burly man rubbed his coarse hands over the girl's body. He saw a flicker in his peripheral vision. The man looked up and saw something that he would never forget.

A hiss erupted from Catalina. The man widened his eyes, and then sat on his hands. Catalina slinked back to her throne. As she sat down, a black cat jumped on her lap and purred.

Two elastic entertainers approached. One was Valentina, sporting a red nighty, which draped over her perky breasts. Her friend was Daniela, a woman with pouty lips painted in black who stood on five-inch heels.

Valentina handed her boss a goblet filled with a deep red concoction. The madam took a sip, and then grimaced.

"This is feeble," she said, handing the drink back.

Suddenly, Catalina lifted her chin and flared her nostrils. Her eyes widen.

"I smell fresh blood," she said as she looked at two businessmen at the entryway.

Barry and Stephen entered the club. Their eyes adjusted to the darkened space.

"What do you think?" Barry asked as he looked at the dancing girl on stage.

"It's dead," Stephen said, gesturing to a chubby woman wearing a witch's hat. "Hey, Barry. There's one for ya."

"What's with the hat?"

"It's Halloween, remember?"

"Don't remind me. Why did we schedule this business trip over the worst holiday?" Barry replied.

"Should we go?" Stephen asked.

As both men turned to leave the deceased dungeon, the scent of sex entered them. Both men followed their senses and saw two creatures skulking their way. The one in red locked eyes with Barry and undressed him with her gaze. Stephen stopped breathing as he watched the lady in black lick her luscious lips.

"Hey, boys. The party's this way," Valentina purred as she caressed Barry's suit.

"You lost?" Daniela muttered, grazing Stephen's groin with her fingertips.

"Uh, not anymore," Stephen said without thinking.

"You have strong hands. Is that your specialty?" Barry asked.

"No. It's sucking," Valentina's hot breath expelled into Barry's ear.

The black cat purred from Catalina's strokes. The queen watched her two best entertainers lead the businessmen by the leashes around their necks. The fetching females entered the VIP Lounge with their catches.

Valentina pushed Barry into a leather chair as he succumbed to her drive. She dangled her silk nighty around his face, messing the part in his boring hairstyle. Her arresting aroma gripped Barry.

Barry let his senses fill with the 100 pounds of goddess in his lap. His heart raced; his breathing intensified; his brain deadened.

Valentina spun, and then oscillated into Barry's groin. He moved with her, left, and then right, back, and then forward. Valentina slid up from his crotch and exhaled onto his cheek. Barry moved his eyes to her neck. There drawn perfectly on her smooth skin was something. He squinted, and then recognized it as a small tattoo of a bat.

Valentina entered his black suit and set aside his tie. Her hand traveled down his white mixed cotton shirt. Barry felt every movement, every inch of her powerful paw. It crossed the bulge in his pants, and then moved to his right pocket. Barry smirked.

"Looking for this?" Barry asked as he removed his wallet from his left pocket.

Valentina smiled as Barry handed her a crisp twenty-dollar bill. She grabbed it, and then kissed Barry's neck.

"You're tasty."

Several chairs away, Daniela handled Stephen with the same conviction. The businessman let his mind go numb. Every thought, every memory of the outside world, erased from his brain. All the thirty-five-year-old father of two could think about was the artist treating him like her masterpiece. Daniela worked on him, teased him. She moved up his body and slowed near his ear. Stephen could hear the faint pop of her tongue as it moistened her lips. He focused all of his energy, all of his senses, on that sound. He craved to do things to this woman that only actions could describe.

The song suddenly changed as Catalina whistled. Daniela grabbed Stephen by his tie.

"Tonight's your lucky night."

Stephen followed her command. He walked toward the woman cloaked in black. As he approached, he saw two figures moving next to him. It was Valentina and his colleague, the man he had forgotten about.

Barry and Stephen stood in front of Catalina as the girls nuzzled them from behind. The two conventioneers flexed their facials muscles into a smirk—facial muscles that only men had. On the outside, these men were by the books, but as they moved deeper into the club, the books closed.

"Hello, boys. Please, sit," the madam instructed. "The name's Catalina. You both from out of town?"

"Does that give us a discount?" Barry asked.

"Don't be coy with me. This is my place."

"Well in that case, are you for sale?" Barry continued.

"You couldn't handle me," Catalina laughed.

Barry pulled out his wallet.

"I'm not interested in your petty cash. However, I am interested in both of you."

Catalina set the feline on the table. Stephen reached to pet it, but it hissed and scurried away. The businessmen watched Catalina reach under the table. She moved slowly as both men held their breath. Finally, she removed two rolled pieces of paper held together by a wax crest shaped into a rabbit. Barry and Stephen accepted them.

"What is it?" Stephen asked.

"An invitation. It's Halloween, you know," Catalina explained.

"Invitation for what, exactly?" Barry said, opening the scroll.

Catalina moved closer to both men. Their bodies froze.

"A night that you'll *never* forget."

Barry caressed the thick, stark-white paper between his fingers. It was as if it were alive, breathing like one of the dancers. He read the top line. "An Invitation to a Special Halloween Masquerade Ball."

"What's the catch?" Stephen asked.

"No catch, except for one thing. You must come in costume. You won't be allowed entry without it. Directions to the location are provided."

"Costume? But it's the middle of the night," Barry said.

"Actually, it's almost sunrise," Stephen chimed in.

"The invitation only stands for one hour. You boys better get going."

Barry felt slippery fingers kneading his neck. He glanced behind him and saw the lights bouncing off Valentina's skin.

"Don't worry. She's just the start."

Barry and Stephen looked at each other, and then shared a nod.

The temperature outside had cooled another two degrees. The only thing alive was the light flashing from the enigmatic gentlemen's club. But then, the front door burst open. Two men with wrinkled suits and tousled hair dashed toward their rental car. Like two teenagers stealing a video game from the rental store, Barry and Stephen worked with precision. All actions happened without speech, without reason. Barry unscrewed the radiator cap, his pain tolerance heightened. Stephen poured two bottles of water in. Then, both men jumped into the car, and then shot through the night.

Stephen drove to a place that he had remembered seeing through binoculars on top of the Stratosphere. It was a humongous sign from an adult boutique that displayed the phrase that both men pined—"24 hours."

Barry and Stephen ran through the store and grabbed cloaks and masks. They paid with cash and made eye contact with no one. As both men stepped from the store with their bags, a cell phone rang, breaking their silence.

"Whose is it?" Stephen asked.

"It's mine," Barry said.

The aroused businessman reached into his suit jacket and read four letters aloud forming a word. They were the last four letters he wanted to see on his phone at the moment—"Home."

"What should I do?" Barry asked.

"Uh. Just answer it."

"But it's so late."

Barry set down the neon pink bag and opened his cell phone.

"Hello?"

He paused.

"Is anything wrong, honey?" he continued.

Barry stared at a sign that read, "All adult toys 20% off."

"It's just that it's so late. Oh. Yes. We are three hours different, remember," Barry chuckled.

Stephen twirled his fingers and squinted his eyes at Barry.

"No. It's okay. The conference was fine. Did the kids have fun trick-or-treating?" Barry asked as a drunk Jesus hollered from the passenger side of a vehicle. "What? Oh. That noise is, uh, the TV. I'm still so sleepy, sweetie. I'm going back to bed. See you soon. I love you."

Barry hung up the phone.

"That was damn close. I shouldn't have answered it."

"What do you think? Will this stuff do?" Stephen asked.

"That's what it says in the invitation," Barry replied. He glanced at his watch. "Shit. We've got twenty minutes."

"I'll let you navigate," Stephen said as both men hustled to the car.

"Remember it's a rental. Just keep it floored."

"But what if it overheats?" Stephen asked.

"I'm willing to take the chance. Aren't you?" Barry said with a smirk.

And then like that, the car raced away. Stephen drove as Barry navigated like two officers in a fighter jet. Creatures still lingering on the Strip didn't distract the men. The car sped past the Las Vegas Sign as they glanced at the warning, "Drive Carefully – Come Back Soon."

Then, the void of night consumed the car as they drove further away from the lights. All of a sudden, desert began to overtake the homes. The minutes passed as the tachometer stayed above four grand. The car turned down a dirt road as any discernable car tracks had vanished. They passed an abandoned mansion.

"This can't be right," Stephen said.

"It says it's at the end of this block," Barry explained, studying the directions.

"But there's nothing out here... Wait," Stephen said.

A single light shined on top of a structure. The car slowed. Its tires crunched on the gravel.

The businessmen stared at the towering mansion. It was three stories tall reaching for the moon. Boards covered its windows. A fallen tree rested on the side of the house. It was like a home for a former member of the Rat Pack, but now, as neglect withered it, the place appeared fit for only a pack of rats.

Barry opened the door and stepped out first; Stephen followed.

"Are you sure this is it? There are no cars?" Stephen quivered.

"I wonder what happened to this place," Barry said.

Barry enjoyed a good show. He knew Las Vegas was full of bizarre clubs and sinful pleasures. While he was nervous, he craved to have a Vegas story to cherish for life.

Stephen, on the other hand, trembled. He was a reserved man by nature. Stephen's idea of sin was having a beer in his basement as his wife yacked on the phone. He remembered a trip he and Barry had taken two years ago to Tampa, Florida. While that conference ended with a stripper in their boss' suite, it lacked the concoction of Las Vegas, Halloween, and a strip club filled with Eastern Europe's finest.

A rusty swing set was in the backyard. "This place is freaking me out," Stephen said.

Barry wandered toward a bucket on the ground. He peered into it and saw something moving. Suddenly, he realized it was a hundred cockroaches covering a piece of meat.

"Holy shit!" Barry barked.

He and Stephen winced.

"I'm outta here! I don't know what's going on!" Stephen exclaimed, running to the car.

"Hold it! It's probably just part of the show," Barry said as he prevented his colleague from leaving.

"I don't care."

"We got one minute left. Let's just play along."

As Stephen removed the car keys from his pocket, he felt something tickle his fingers. He looked down and saw it was a long piece of string. At first, Stephen thought it was just a thread from his suit, but as he studied it closer, he realized it was a strand of his wife's flowing blonde hair that had followed him all this way. His stomach turned as his conscience questioned his actions.

"Let's head back to the hotel. We have an early flight tomorrow," Stephen reasoned.

Barry put his hand on Stephen's back.

"We've come this far. Think of those girls at the club."

Barry's words killed Stephen's conscience. He stopped his escape, put the keys back into his pocket, and then wiped his hands.

Both men grabbed the contents of their pink bags. They had seconds to don their outfits and arrive at the door holding their invitations. Stephen flung his cloak around his jacket and positioned a black half-mask onto his face, assuming the identity of a singer from some twisted opera.

Barry chose the full disguise; a white porcelain mask concealed his identity. He too added a cloak, and then led the way to the start of the night's end.

Stephen and Barry lurked around the house. They moved delicately through the shadows as their new identities had given them the confidence they so desperately sought. Their hands no longer trembled as they grasped the white scroll that gave them power. As they made it around the lifeless house, the entryway presented itself. It was a sturdy door made of metal, which was in contrast to the otherwise shabby house. And whatever lay behind it, needed protection. Both men stopped at the rabbit head made into a knocker.

"What do we do now?" Stephen asked.

"Knock twice, pause, then three times."

Stephen followed the order, each pound of his knuckles sending vibrations through his body. Then, the sound of silence screamed.

"This is a joke. Let's get outta here," Stephen said.

Barry and Stephen turned to leave, but as they removed their eyes from the stout door, a creak hit their ears. They turned as the door squeaked open. A creature well over six feet tall poked his head out. A black and white Venetian mask frozen with a glare greeted the men.

"Yes," the masked man said with a deep voice.

"We're, uh, here for the party?" Barry said without his usual arrogance.

"Party? This is not a party."

Both men stopped. Then, Stephen remembered the thick parchment between his fingers. He showed the item to the doorman. "We have this."

"Ah... The invitation. Please, come in," the man said.

The masked man opened the door. The house sucked in Barry and Stephen. Candles flickered off the rotted wood, which was covered with cobwebs. Soft medieval music out of a silent horror movie filled the house. A smell they couldn't place hit them. It was like a mix of mothballs and burnt toast.

Barry and Stephen slithered past the entryway and into the kitchen. They saw two masked partiers filling glasses with a deep red concoction. As the businessmen approached, the beings stopped and stared. Barry nodded. Then, the two returned the gesture.

Barry and Stephen coasted into the attached living room. The music seemed to intensify yet they couldn't discern where it originated. Five camouflaged creatures mellowed on a long couch. Exotic Venetian disguises concealed their identities, except for two young women wearing only half masks. Their exposed breasts captivated the crowd. Flames from the candles flickered off their supple skin and massaged the eyes of their voyeurs. Everyone in the room watched the ladies embrace. The women licked and groped like there was no tomorrow, and for all Barry and Stephen knew, there wasn't. While emotionless stares emanated from the businessmen's masks, the pores on their faces filled with sweat.

Stephen felt his muscles twinge. He squirmed as a board under his suede, size 10 loafers squeaked. Everyone turned to the stimulated man as if the music had stopped.

"Welcome, boys, to our ball!" Catalina roared, redirecting the room's focus.

Barry and Stephen tracked the voice up the stairs at the end of the room. There stood the queen of the night, a half-mask cloaking her face. She stepped down the stairway with her arms open. Barry took her hand and kissed it with his porcelain lips. Stephen followed his partner, but his mask offered her his real flesh.

"Please, let me bring you some place a bit more private," she proposed.

Catalina climbed up the stairs.

"This place is too bizarre, man," Stephen whispered to Barry, eyeing all the eyes on him.

"It's our last night in Vegas. Tomorrow we'll be back home in the cold. Just roll with it," Barry muttered.

The guys ascended the stairway; the aged wood barked with each step. The upstairs hallway greeted them with gloom. More cobwebs dangled over their heads. Candles bounced off the confined hallway. The mysterious smell hit them again.

"What is that smell?" Barry asked.

"I don't know. But these cobwebs look real. Are you sure this is just a Halloween party?"

Before Barry could respond, Catalina reached into both men's cloaks.

"Have we a night for you," she said, yanking their ties.

Catalina tugged Barry's noose just enough to show him his destiny. It was a dark bedroom housing a half-masked being. Barry hesitated leaving his confidant. But as he focused on the room's occupant, the color red clawed his cones—the same color that brought him there in the first place. It was Valentina.

Barry reached for his wallet—a gesture of his enlarging ego.

"That won't save you," Catalina laughed.

Barry looked as his friend one last time before he entered.

"Good luck, man. I hope I won't catch you balancing the woman's checkbook," Barry joked.

And then like that, the room inhaled him. Barry glided toward the beauty surrounded by candles. It was as if she were another flame, burning the brightest on the satin sheets. An arresting aroma flowed over him. It was the scent of another female. The door shut behind him as his attention shifted to the origin of his senses—a slippery six feet of sex. Her name was Natasha and just like the tallest flower in the garden, she used her height to dominate the insects that tasted her.

"Let us give you a little show to get you warmed up," Natasha said as she sauntered to Valentina.

Both women embraced with a kiss, and then turned their sloe eyes toward Barry. He could see the fire flickering in them.

Down the hall, Catalina guided Stephen. She liked the quiet ones, the ones who absorbed everything rather than expelled it. She opened the door to another bedroom. A cool breeze hit Stephen. He couldn't speak, couldn't think. Stephen stepped inside the room and saw a creature wrapped in a shroud. Stephen slowed, but then he saw the five-inch heels poking out of the bottom. He knew who it was.

Daniela exposed herself to the room. Her plump breasts filled Stephen's stare.

"Get this boy ready," Catalina instructed.

With that, Daniela stood up and grabbed the lost businessman by his tie. She pushed him on the bed and moved to the beat of the music filling the room from downstairs. Stephen let her fingers work on him. She removed his mask and unfastened his cape. His eyes fixed on a pair of dice painted on the ceiling. He wondered how many other lost travelers had rested their eyes on the number seven.

Daniela kissed his cheek. Stephen focused all of his attention on the softest lips he had ever felt. She licked him, which cooled his face, and then blew her breath, chilling him. Stephen wanted to look into her eyes. He wanted to see the image of beauty. But as he locked eyes with hers, they appeared dark, evil. Stephen pulled back and saw two fangs jutting from her mouth. She plunged for his neck.

"No! I want his blood!" Catalina demanded.

Daniela flew off him. He clamored back. Then, he stared at Catalina—the madam, the woman of the night, the vampire. She opened her mouth. Stephen froze. The businessman thought about his family. He wondered how he had lost his way from the light. But that was all hindsight now as he faced something incomprehensible, yet at the same time, bizarrely erotic.

Catalina lunged at Stephen. She sunk her fangs deep into his neck. Two lines of blood trickled down his skin and saturated his white dress shirt. Stephen yelled louder than he had ever yelled. Catalina removed her teeth and licked her lips. Then, she went in for another bite.

In the next bedroom, the mask-less Barry heard Stephen's yell. He smirked. The two vixens licked Barry's neck with passion. His eyes rolled back as his hands filled with one breast of each lady. One was larger than the other, filling his hands just a little more. But both were softer than silk and warmer than fresh bread. The nipple in his left hand poked his wedding ring. He teased the breast in his right hand, which finally hardened.

Suddenly, the door burst open.

"Out! I want him all to myself," Catalina shouted.

Valentina and Natasha sprang from their places and scurried out. Barry felt the cold surround him. But then, Catalina's eyes burned into him igniting a new flame.

"So, are you having fun?"

"Well, now that you're here," Barry said with overconfidence.

"Little boy, you can't handle me," Catalina laughed.

"You wanna bet?"

He stood up and gravitated toward her. He studied her long nails, and her flowing black hair aglow with the flicker of the candles. Barry noticed her skin appeared warmer, more alive, and filled with blood. As he approached, her aroma engulfed him, a scent he would never forget. Barry stopped and looked at the color red smeared around her mouth. But before he could ask, she clutched him and thrust him to the wall.

"You're gonna taste good," Catalina whispered, nibbling on his ear.

Barry's mind went numb. The pain in his ear only intensified his lust. He prepared for the most intense moment of his night, a time that built up to his climax. Catalina pulled back. Barry glanced at her, but what he saw was something not even the thirty-seven-year-old college educated businessman could have predicted.

Fangs protruded from Catalina's mouth. She attacked Barry's naked neck. He closed his eyes preparing for it, anticipating the pain, but then someone pounded on the door. Catalina removed her focus from Barry as the door opened.

"It's almost daylight," the masked man mouthed.

"This won't take long," Catalina said.

The door shut. Catalina returned to bite Barry. He stood at the back wall, the furthest point in the confined room. He noticed a painting hanging. It was Catalina wearing a sinful dress. She sat on a throne with fangs jutting from her mouth. Her hand grasped a glass of red liquid. Barry read the date marked in the corner, "1681."

The hungry vampire prowled toward him from behind. She opened her mouth, but then Barry ducked. She lunged at the painting, knocking it down. Barry jumped on the bed. She charged at him. He dove off the side, using the bed for protection. He moved left; she moved right. He swayed right; she leaned left. Barry waited, his heart pounding. She sensed his flowing blood. Catalina leaped at him. Barry grabbed her in the air and threw her on the bed. He darted toward the door.

Barry exploded into the hall and slammed the door shut. He hustled toward the next bedroom, Stephen's room. He opened the door. There she was, Daniela, kissing his partner's neck.

"Stephen?" Barry said, but silence returned.

Barry entered slowly, softly. As he approached Stephen, he saw his colleague's eyes rolled back. He was grunting. Barry didn't know if he was enjoying it or detesting it. But as he stepped toward the foot of the bed, Daniela whipped around, blood oozing out of her mouth. She bit at Barry, cutting the tie from his neck. He stumbled back and dove through the doorway. Barry hurled the door shut leaving his business associate, his colleague, and his friend of six years. Barry realized he was all alone now, all alone in a house that didn't even exist.

Barry vaulted into another bedroom. Candles filled the space as Barry searched the room for something, for anything. He opened a dresser, drawer by drawer. A cryptic white mask lay next to a collection of adult toys. Barry donned the new persona.

"Have you seen the subject?" the voice of Catalina asked.

Barry turned and saw the woman of the night standing at the doorway. He tried to control his heart, tried to silence its pounding.

"Our guest? Have you seen him?" Catalina continued.

The masked Barry shook his head.

"Well, get downstairs," she said, leaving Barry alone.

His trick had worked, but the problem now was the crowd of creatures underneath his feet. Barry ran to the only window in the room, but boards covered it not letting anything in, or in Barry's case, not letting anyone out.

Barry sneaked to the door. He peeked out and saw the deserted hallway. He made his way to the stairs. A mask popped up from the shadows. Barry wavered. The masked being studied him, but then continued through the hallway. Barry was free. He tiptoed down each stair. He clutched the wall, covered in cobwebs. While there were only 15 stairs, they were 15 opportunities for his feet to expose him.

Finally, Barry reached the ground floor, the floor of the exit door. He had to make it through the living room. Barry looked at the path out. Through the murkiness, he saw the metallic front door, but also a dozen monsters. He started his trek. He didn't know what he would say when he reached the exit, but all he cared about was that door. Barry focused on the stout metal fifteen feet away from him. Suddenly, a mask frozen with a smirk invaded on his right. Then, another floated to his left. The music seemed to intensify. Masked fiends pushed him around. One shrieked. Another laughed. A third howled. Breasts gyrated around him. He waited for a monster to grab him, to expose him to the room.

Someone stomped down the stairs. The beings turned. Barry focused on the door. He was only five feet away.

"Silence! Against the wall! All of you!" Catalina yelled.

Barry halted. He watched as the group obeyed. Barry contemplated running, but he knew that stealth was his last weapon. He assumed his place in the line as Catalina paced like a hungry drill sergeant.

"I know one of you is an imposter. Step forward!"

Barry remained still.

"This is your last chance," Catalina warned.

The crowd stood mute. All that Barry could do now was wait. Catalina shifted to the masked being on the end. She yanked its mask off as a handsome man with fangs gawked back. She moved to the next one and snatched its mask. A female vampire hissed. Then, Catalina moved to a white mask—Barry's mask. She stopped as time seemed to slow. Barry shuddered. Catalina leaned in to him slowly.

"I can smell your fresh blood," she whispered, sending chills down his spine.

She painted his cloak with her finger, and then slid her claw up to his chin. This was it. Barry held his breath. He thought about his trip, his family, and his life. Through the darkness, he could see the light that they represented. But then, Barry realized it was not some illusion of light, but an actual ray of sunlight piercing through the seam of a boarded window. The beam cut through the void in the room and rested on the wall behind Barry. Catalina stopped. The room froze. This was Barry's only chance.

He shoved the vamp aside and dashed past her. Barry's mask flew off. He sprinted toward the light. He heard shrieks behind him, but he couldn't look back. Barry dove through the air and crashed through the withered wood. He rolled on the ground as the rising sun showered him. Catalina and two vampires stood at the opening. The sun burned their skin. They screeched, stopped by the light.

Barry glanced back for a brief moment and saw the hungry creatures burning him with their eyes. But then, he tossed his cloak off and rushed toward the rental car. Barry pulled the handle, but it was locked. He patted his crumpled suit jacket and his disheveled pants. Barry realized he didn't have the keys.

"Stephen," he mouthed as he looked back at the towering mansion.

Barry took off down the street. All he cared about was running toward the only thing he could see—the sun.

Darkness still filled the second bedroom of the prominent house. Catalina slithered inside. A boil scarred her once feminine face. She locked eyes with Valentina, Daniela, Natasha, and the new addition to her private club—Stephen.

"Your friend got away," Catalina said.

Stephen looked at the floor. He reached for a wallet—Barry's wallet. He removed an airplane ticket and showed it to his new friends. Catalina smiled and laughed devilishly, filling the house, and the street, with an evil cackle.

We need to find Barry tonight. That's the gig I was talking about. We're here now. Let's go to meet my friends. They're inside and we don't even need an invitation. But before I bring you in, I have to show you something. Do you like my fangs? This will only hurt for a bit. Hahahaha!